THE

GLOVEMAKER'S

WAR

THE

GLOVEMAKER'S

WAR

KATHERINE WILLIAMS

atmosphere press

For Violet and Beatrix

"What the heart has once owned and had, it shall never lose."
Henry Ward Beecher

PROLOGUE

I t was time to go. *The Allied invasion of France had begun,
and Luc would join his comrades in the Resistance at
daybreak in the nearby mountains. Through the only window
of the hideaway, he could see the fading moon low in the sky.
Pale and watery, it sneaked out intermittently from behind the
drifting clouds, casting strange shadows on the floor of the
barn. In the darkness of the outbuilding, the animals were
slowly waking one by one, stirred by a circadian rhythm over
which they had no control. Running his finger over Eve's cheek,
he kissed her gently and breathed in her essence, trying to
preserve her in his memory forever. She smiled in her sleep and
touched his arm. He felt for his clothes on the floor and
wrestled on his torn pants, then yanked a ragged sweater over
his head. He had never felt such heartache. He wanted to stay
in the safe house with her forever, but it was his duty to fight
for his country.*

*He crept quietly across the barn to where he could make
out Eve's leather bag in the muddy light. He knew it was where
she kept her glove form and glove-making supplies—the
contrivances of her disguise as a courier for the Resistance. He
rummaged for the rose-colored gloves that she'd made for*

3

herself and treasured so much. He pressed one against his cheek, before tucking it close to his heart in the top pocket of his jacket. Then he found the glove form and brushing his lips across the crumpled paper on which he'd written a message the night before, he pushed the note deep inside a hollow finger of the metal mold.

Overcome with emotion, he stumbled to the door and opened it. Tears trickled down his cheeks and he wiped them on his rough jacket sleeve. The misty gloom of the early morning enveloped him, and without looking back, he was gone.

CHAPTER 1

GEORGINA
Manhattan, 2016

I t was late April in the Northeast, when dandelion clocks are known to fly, but wintry puffs were blowing around instead. Georgina leaned her head back, letting the icy flakes land on her eyelids and tickle her nose, wondering how something so beautiful and silent could cause so much chaos. The snow had been falling steadily for a couple of hours, the brashness and hubbub of the city's streets temporarily muffled under a feathery white eiderdown. Cars glided like slow-moving igloos, their tires skidding on the slushy surface, while shoppers in heavy boots and thick parkas lumbered between frosty hillocks dumped on the sidewalks. Georgina, however, had no intention of walking anywhere. An eager cabbie spotted her jubilant wave and quickly veered across two lanes of traffic, his car snaking from side to side, throwing up sheets of sleet in its wake. It took some time, but the indomitable New Yorker prevailed, prodded by an authority that the wealthy always seem to command.

"The Plaza Grand on Lexington, please."

The driver turned to look at her, breathing in the luxuriousness of her perfume. "For you, I'd drive to the end of the earth," he thought. He set off again, down 5th Avenue, like a fearless knight battling with cars to his left and to his right.

Enveloped in the warmth of the taxi, Georgina hugged herself. The risky chauffeuring and muted mayhem outside her window didn't faze her. It was an entirely perfect day. Her cheeks glowed with excitement, almost matching the delicate pink of her beanie hat and leather gloves. Visions of a victory celebration popped into her head. "Yes, I'll have a party at that new nightclub that Scarlett told me about. I deserve it."

Her presentation to investors had gone very well. Enlisting her friends' expertise had yielded dividends. Lily, who headed up a creative agency, had helped her with the pitch deck, and Jen had agreed to merchandise the product. The investors loved that Jen's cool cosmetics company donated proceeds of sales to environmental and social causes. Georgina's concept of a quinoa facial scrub, discovered on a trip to Peru, was now on track to becoming a retail reality.

After a slow journey across town, the cab pulled up in front of the hotel. The doorman slid out into the street to open the passenger door.

"Welcome home, Miss Smytheson. Nice weather for polar bears!"

"I love it, George. The city has a dreamlike quality today. Are you feeling better?"

"All the better for seeing you. If all our guests were like you, my job would be a breeze."

"I've been worried about you."

"Just had a wisdom tooth removed, that's all."

She reached into her bag for the box of Krispy Kreme donuts that she'd bought on her way to the presentation.

"For you. I know they're your favorite."

"I can't believe you remembered! You're the best. I'll have

to eat them before I get home, though. The wife has me on a low-carb diet."

"It's our little secret," she smiled.

A gust of heat hit them as he opened the door to the lobby, ushering her inside with an exaggerated flourish. Georgina swept past him into the hotel, the heels of her boots clicking on the polished marble floor toward the penthouse elevator. Removing her hat with one hand, she punched her special code into the keypad with the other. The doors purred as they welcomed her in, then closed behind her, sealing her privilege. After a brief ride, they opened again onto the small hallway of the suite where she lived with her mother.

She shrugged off her fur-trimmed puffer coat and threw it carelessly on the entry table. Settling into a plush, upholstered armchair, she peeled off a rose-colored kid-glove finger by finger and, marveling at the softness of the leather, brushed it against her cheek. Gloves had always been her weakness, something her mother had never understood. She tilted her head to one side as she ran her fingers through her highlighted hair, crossing her long legs at the ankles. Looking down, she was dismayed to see salt stains on the fine Italian leather of her boots.

Her view of the Manhattan skyline from high up on the sixty-third floor was usually marvelous, the colors of the sky constantly changing, shifting, casting kaleidoscopic shapes and shadows on the building opposite. But today, dense, snow-filled clouds hovered near the windows, blocking out all possibilities of wonder. She wasn't going to let that spoil her joy. Her mother was away; she had the apartment to herself. Perhaps Marco would stop by later to help her celebrate. Just thinking of him made her shiver with desire.

The hotel had been Georgina's home since her parents' divorce eighteen years ago. Her mother, Angela Harrison, was from a French-British family in England and had met Georgina's father, Charles Smytheson III, at a dinner party in London in the late '70s. He was in the wine business, passing through London on his way back to New York after a tasting tour of Burgundy, and Angela worked as a bilingual secretary for the prestigious wine dealers Bailey Brothers and Walker. The hostess cleverly sat them beside each other; he dazzled her with exotic travel stories, while she won him over with her European charm. By the end of the meal, they'd fallen in love. He swept her away to his apartment on Central Park West with promises of a thrilling life in America.

But the glamour of their Manhattan lifestyle faded when Georgina was born. Mothering, Angela discovered, was not her strong suit. They enrolled Georgina in a boarding school in England, believing she'd have more companionship there and the discipline they'd neither the time nor the inclination to provide. Lonely without her daughter for company, Angela became unhappy with a husband who was always away. She was curious as to why Charles spent so much time traveling. She did a bit of snooping and discovered an affair. It was the end of their marriage. Charles, feeling guilty for his infidelity to both his wife and daughter and needing to move on to his new life with a clear conscience, set up generous trust funds in both their names.

Charles now lived on his vineyard in Oregon with a much younger wife called Petra and their son, Ben. Georgina rarely heard from him these days. There was the odd phone call, hastily made from airports, always when he was traveling alone, out of earshot of his new family. Georgina felt like a snapshot in a photo album, to be shelved away and only taken out to look at in nostalgic moments.

She recognized that she was the product of her father's guilt-money. Although she enjoyed partying and trips to

Aspen or the Hamptons with her high-flying friends, she didn't buy into her mother's lifestyle of constant holiday. She'd glimpsed inside Angela's hollow shell and decided she needed more. She liked to work to keep herself busy and feel some semblance of self-worth. This new business venture was important to her: it could mean independence.

Her cell phone vibrated from the depths of her bag. Rummaging for a few seconds, she pulled it out, peered at the message on the screen, and groaned, tossing it back. Her mum was probably freaking out about her summer Hamptons rental and wanted Georgina to call the realtor to check that the deposit went through. While on a cruise in the Mediterranean, she was already thinking about her next trip, her next "bit of fun." Even when Georgina was alone, her mother could still suffocate her with her vanity.

She couldn't deal with these shenanigans now. She needed a drink.

The lounge was Georgina's favorite room in the hotel. Ornamental trees lined the cavernous space, their sparkly lights reflecting in the highly polished floors and evoking an ambiance of perpetual Christmas. She spotted him in deep conversation with an attractive woman dressed in a slick fitted suit, seated on a leather bar stool. They were leaning into each other as if their exchange was for their ears only. Then the shrill of the businesswoman's laughter rose above the buzz of conversation in the room; she touched Marco's arm and looked up at him, her smile dazzling in the shiny atmosphere. Georgina shrank behind an oversized arrangement of purple lilacs, letting the heady scent of spring waft over her, and stumbled towards an empty seat, trying to understand what she'd just witnessed.

He appeared silently at her side, his discreet cough

KATHERINE WILLIAMS

interrupting her thoughts. He carried a silver tray, balancing a pink cocktail glass, which he placed on the table beside her. Reaching for the drink, Georgina removed the slice of lime, accidentally brushing his hand as she did so. She blushed slightly, remembering where she liked him to touch her.

"How did you know I was here?" she asked him. She took a sip of the perfectly chilled Cosmopolitan, her blue eyes wide and questioning.

"I always know when you're around," he whispered. His lips turned up at the corners, his eyes twinkling, as he bowed with a flourish and backed away. As Marco returned to the bar, she noted how his buttocks moved in his tight black pants. She loved the thrill their clandestine hook-ups and flirtatious exchanges gave her, but right now suspicious thoughts had taken over her usual carefree disposition.

The text message she'd ignored earlier flashed again on the screen. She sighed and read it: *"Grandy isn't well. Got message from her doctor to say that she's asking for me. You'll have to go. I'm sure you'll manage until I get back. Will call in a few days to see how you're getting on. Mum X."*

It wasn't the message Georgina had been expecting at all. She hadn't seen her grandmother for years. She was concerned her mother assumed she would take care of everything. But the fact that she didn't want to cut short her cruise for her sick mother only highlighted the selfishness that Georgina had come to expect. As a child, Georgina had rarely seen her mother when she was away at boarding school. Angela had always been too busy to visit, even for important events. When she was eleven Georgina had learned to cover up her disappointment with bravado, but the painful memory that she'd long since tried to forget, now came to mind. That year she'd won a prize for 'Most Improved' in her class. Thrilled, she'd written to her mother to tell her the prize was to be given out on Speech Day and that she really wanted her to be there. But Angela let her down, her excuse being that she had a critical

10

meeting to attend. Instead, it was her grandmother who sat proudly in the audience as Georgina went up to receive the engraved silver cup.

As Georgina sipped her cocktail, a picture of a gentle, dark-haired woman floated into her mind. She remembered that her grandmother had always been the one to visit, before their get-togethers ended unexpectedly. With no explanation at all, her mum had one day ordered the school not to allow meetings between grandmother and granddaughter. It was as if she'd wanted to erase their English history from their lives. Her grandmother had continued to phone her though. Even if it was a tenuous relationship, it had been better than nothing.

But she couldn't recall when she'd last spoken with Grandy. Communication was tricky, especially with an old lady who went to bed a seven o'clock in the evening on the other side of the Atlantic. It must have been at least fifteen years since they'd last met. That the doctor had been in contact left her feeling uneasy. There had to be something very seriously wrong with her grandmother for her mum to make this unusual request.

Georgina let out a sigh. "Oh, but it's such bad timing," she thought. She felt her phone vibrate again. It was a message from her friend Tilly, asking if she wanted to join her at the opening of a new nightclub that night. Tilly, an influencer who was being paid to feature the club on her Facebook page, needed as many high rollers to attend as possible. Georgina wrestled with the pros and cons in her head before reluctantly shooting her friend a quick text: "Thanks but can't. Off to London." She then pressed the British Airways app on her phone to check on the flight times. There was one leaving Kennedy at nine-thirty that night, which would get her into Heathrow the following morning. There were just two seats left in First Class. She took a deep breath, then clicked "Book." Her mother would have to pay her back later if she couldn't be bothered to interrupt her holiday.

"I haven't been to London or seen Camilla for ages. And when I've made sure Grandy is okay, I could check out that branding agency that Lily recommended, too," she thought.

She glanced down at her watch, its diamonds glistening back at her. It was two o'clock in the afternoon: she had plenty of time to get packed and be at the airport by seven-thirty. She waved over to Marco, signaling for another drink. He winked at her as he set down the pink cocktail on her side table, together with a small bowl of edamame.

"How did the meeting go this morning?' he asked softly.

"It was great. Would you like to help me celebrate now? I won't be able to see you later tonight—I have to fly to London. My grandmother isn't well." Popping a salty bean into her mouth, she ran the tip of her tongue over her glossy lips and smiled up at him with hungry eyes.

As they lounged on the king-sized bed, she rolled over onto her stomach and twisted the sheet around her naked body, balancing her head on her hand.

"Who was that I saw you chatting to earlier?" she asked.

"It was Luisa Rivera, the editor from First Time Publishing. She was in the hotel for a conference. She just stopped by the bar to tell me that they like my manuscript. You remember, I told you about the new publishing company that's specializing in Hispanic writers."

"Oh, that's who she was. She's hot." Georgina gulped. "That's amazing. Good for you."

Marco ruffled her hair. "You've turned quite green! Do you think I have something going on with her?"

"You know I'm not the jealous type." She punched his arm. "You're a free agent."

"Well, she was very interested in me, I'll have you know, but not like you're thinking. This is the break I need. Now, tell me what happened with your pitch?"

"They weren't interested at first. They said the market was flooded with eco-friendly products like mine, but then I reeled them in with the connection I have with Jen's new sustainable cosmetics company. They loved the social and environmental component." She flashed a self-satisfied smile. "It was like an episode of Shark Tank."

"Well done, you! How long will you be away?" he asked, nuzzling his nose into her hair. She could feel his warm breath on her neck as she leaned back into him.

"I have no idea. I guess until my mother finishes her cruise, which isn't for another two weeks. I have so much to do with my new project, but I really have to go."

"Well, I hope you'll be back for my sister's birthday in May. She's planning a party and my mother wants to meet you."

Georgina swallowed hard as she pushed herself away from him. She sat upright against the pillows, pulling up the sheet to cover herself before folding her arms across her body. "I don't think that's a good idea," she said slowly. "Don't you like things the way they are? Introducing me to your family is just going to complicate everything." Something her friend Scarlett said kept rattling around in her head: "Look, it's OK to shag him. But don't let things get too serious. The minute he suggests meeting his family, run the other way. He'll be proposing next and cashing in big time. Cha-ching!" She didn't know whether to believe that he was after her money. She was far more uneasy about another word, which began with a capital C: Commitment. She liked things the way they were. Marriage was simply not on her radar.

She couldn't help but stare at Marco as he got out of bed. At thirty-four, his thick black hair was lightly peppered with gray, and early-morning workouts had honed his naturally toned physique. He bent down to reach for his pants.

"Why does it always come to this with you? What are you scared of? You think the idea of introducing me to your friends as a writer is cool, but whenever I suggest meeting my family, you get cold feet. This isn't the first time. You're pathetic. You live in your posh hotel and me in a walk-up in the Bronx with my mother. I get it. It's not going to work, is it?"

He shrugged on the jacket of his waiter's uniform. "I've got work to do."

Georgina saw something in his handsome face that she'd never seen before. His soft brown eyes, which usually sparkled at her, now flashed in anger.

"I don't know what you're saying. You know I've never thought of you like that. I love being with you. My friends really like you too. Why do we have to take things to another level when they're great as they are? We've never argued before. Let's not do this just before I leave."

"We've never argued before because, if you haven't noticed, we always do things your way. I can't do this anymore. Have fun in London." He looked back at her as he opened the door. "And you're right, Luisa is hot."

Later that evening, the snow was collecting in drifts as quickly as it was being cleared.

"Can't you go any faster?" Georgina shouted to the driver from the back seat of her limousine.

"Sorry, Miss, but we're not going anywhere right now." He took his hands off the steering wheel, throwing them up in the air in frustration. Georgina clicked the airline app on her phone. Her flight number popped up automatically, indicating that it was delayed.

"Well, it doesn't matter."

Sinking her head further back into the softness of her seat, she closed her eyes, her mind drifting back to a few hours earlier. She could hear an echo of Marco's sexy voice murmuring to her, remembering how his touch had made her

14

quiver with pleasure. She shivered. Their parting was strained and angry; she didn't want to hurt him, but he'd hurt her too. She simply liked things the way they were, but he'd gone and ruined that.

It was eight-thirty when they finally reached the airport terminal, almost an hour later than the recommended check-in time.

The clerk glanced at Georgina's passport.

"Good evening, Miss Smytheson. I'm afraid your flight is delayed due to the weather, and we're not sure at this time when it'll be leaving. Please wait in the lounge until you hear any announcements."

As a well-heeled traveler, Georgina had her routine: passing through the specially designated security lane, she went straight for Duty-Free to pick up some of her favorite make-up and perfume. She then made her way to the first-class lounge, thinking that she would find a quiet booth to have dinner; but her plans were thwarted. The lounge was overflowing with anxious passengers scrutinizing the silent scene outside the vast picture windows of the terminal. Georgina realized that there was no point in worrying. She was lucky to find a seat at the bar, where she asked for a glass of champagne while catching up with messages. It was going to be a long wait; at least the prospect of her first-class seat that turned into a bed comforted her.

She noticed that the handsome businessman seated next to her had just turned his head her way. She positioned herself to get a better look at him and tilted her head to one side, her lips pouting.

"Where are you off to?"

"I have a meeting in Manchester tomorrow morning, but that doesn't look likely to be happening now. I'm Alex, by the way," he said, offering her his hand.

She took in his chiseled face, with its dark designer stubble, admiring the way his eyes crinkled at the corners as he smiled at her. He was exactly the type she usually lusted after. Dipping the tip of a manicured finger into her glass, she licked off the chilled champagne, putting Marco firmly out of mind.

It was almost twenty-four hours later when she finally boarded her flight to London. The delay had started to feel like a bad omen. Her mother had given her absolutely no details of her grandmother's condition; the old lady might even be dead by the time she got there. She wasn't sure she could handle her grandmother's passing away on her own.

The hushed atmosphere in the first-class cabin was soothing, with soft music playing in the background as the cabin crew went through the take-off procedures. As soon as the seat belt sign was switched off, a steward appeared with a pair of pajamas, a comforter, sheets, and another glass of champagne. He reclined her seat as she stood in the aisle. When he'd gone, she lay back, cocooned in the soft comforter. She closed her eyes, trying to stop the swimming sensation in her head. Airsickness wasn't something that usually affected her. At first, she put it down to a lack of sleep, and to drinking far too much fizz, which airlines use as a panacea for all that ails their disgruntled first-class passengers. But now there were also flutters multiplying in her stomach. The nervous anticipation of what she would find, when she finally reached her grandmother's house in Worcester, was growing.

CHAPTER 2

GEORGINA AND EVE
Worcester, England, 2016

The black and white building in Friars Lane had rested there for centuries, its foundation settled into a rickety shape, like the bones of an arthritic old man bowing under the weight of time. It sat at the end of a row of homes with roofs of different heights, all leaning into each other for support, and looking delicately balanced, like a tower of playing cards that could topple with the push of a finger. Red and white tulips stood to attention in black iron pots that lined the sidewalk, and baskets filled with showy spring flowers hung from metal hooks on the wooden framework of the houses. Cars lined the narrow street, forcing the Uber driver to double park. Georgina got out and wheeled her suitcase to number thirty-two.

A large picture window to the left of the front door was shuttered from the inside, preventing passersby from peering in, and giving the impression that no one was at home. Georgina ducked under the eaves and looked for a doorbell, catching her head on the lintel; she didn't remember the house being quite so small. From its resting place on the front door, a lion's head made of brass stared at her. Tentatively she took the lion's mouth in her hand; it felt heavy as she thumped on the hard wood. Moments later she heard a rustling sound from inside.

"It's Georgina Smytheson. I've come to see my grandmother," she shouted through the closed door.

"I don't think Miss Harrison is expecting anyone," a voice replied.

"Didn't my mother phone to tell you that I'd be coming? I've had a long journey from New York. Do you think you could let me in?"

As she stood waiting on the doorstep, a whining noise coming from further up the street distracted her. A milk cart was making its way down the middle of the road. The milkman jumped out, grabbed the empty bottle from the doorstep, winked at her, and thrust a full one into her hand. As he turned to leave, a woman of about fifty opened the front door. She was wearing a long cardigan pulled over a navy nurse's uniform, her untamed frizzy hair springing free from a hastily styled ponytail. "Eve is still asleep. I was just getting dressed. Come in."

"I can't believe they still deliver milk. I thought that had died out years ago," Georgina said.

"It's all the rage now. Organic milk delivered right to your doorstep." The nurse took the milk bottle from Georgina's outstretched hand.

Picking up her suitcase, Georgina held her breath as she entered the house for the first time in almost fifteen years. Her mother had always been embarrassed by the shop she grew up living in and had only brought Georgina here a few times as a child. Even though it would have been a far more convenient place to spend weekend breaks from school, Georgina always spent time with Camilla's family, or in Angela's flat in

London, rather than with her grandmother.

The nurse, who said her name was Eileen, cracked open the white-painted shutters to let the morning light stream in through the slats and brighten up the living area. As Georgina looked around the cleverly converted space, she spotted some pieces of mid-century furniture that some of her jet-set friends would pay a fortune for. Two beech armchairs, designed by the famous furniture maker Lucian Ercolani, flanked a matching coffee table. An island, covered with stacks of artfully arranged books and magazines, looked like it was once a shop's counter. The home was calm and inviting as she remembered, and not at all dingy as her mother liked to describe it.

"I'm sure you're ready for a cup of tea after your long journey," Eileen said. "I'll just put the kettle on. Make yourself comfortable."

"I'd rather have coffee," Georgina said. She shook off her jacket and thrust it into the nurse's hand.

"I'll see what I can rustle up for you, dear. Your grandmother doesn't drink coffee, but I keep a jar of instant for myself. Milk and sugar?" Eileen took the jacket, putting Georgina's brusqueness down to jetlag.

Georgina just nodded and looked around her. "How is my grandmother?" Georgina asked when Eileen returned with a mug.

"She's comfortable. Well, she has her good days and her bad ones. She's been having breathing issues, which is why I'm here. I've put an egg on to boil for you too—you must be hungry after that long flight." She went back into the kitchen, returning after a few minutes with a soft-boiled egg in an eggcup and a slice of toast on a small plate. "Pull up a stool. It's not for me to tell you to make yourself at home—you're family after all. I'll take Eve's breakfast up to her and tell her you're here."

Georgina took a sip of the pale, watery coffee. She heaved a sigh. It tasted awful. She pushed it to one side and took a bite of toast.

Eve lay in bed beneath the open upstairs window listening to the sounds filtering in. She heard someone whistling in the alleyway behind the house, the crunch of footsteps, low murmurs of voices, then laughter and the whine of the milk cart. The twittering of a song thrush each morning, mixed with the other familiar sounds, set a comforting rhythm to her life.

She thought she could hear someone knocking at the front door, but she couldn't be sure.

These days sleep came laced with dreams of past times that Eve had long since shut from her mind; not flights of fancy that evaporated before waking, but vivid memories of people and events. It seemed as though they hung around for a reason; distant recollections kept tugging her back and didn't want to let go. She needed to share those memories that she had buried so deep for so long before they were lost forever.

Tiredness was her nemesis and it exasperated her when she couldn't stay awake for long enough to gather her thoughts. She was nodding off again when Eileen came in with her breakfast tray. The nurse quietly placed the tray on the bedside table before checking on the level of Eve's oxygen tank. Eve opened her eyes as Eileen lightly lifted her forward, plumping up her pillows.

"Good morning. How are you today?"

Eve opened her eyes and smiled weakly at her nurse. "Oh, just hunky-dory," she said. "Did I hear someone at the door, dear, was it the milkman? I need to pay him."

"Yes, you did hear someone, but it wasn't Len. I have a

lovely surprise for you. Your granddaughter Georgina is here to see you."

Eve looked puzzled. "Georgina? She can't be here. She lives in America. I haven't seen her for years. Are you sure it's not my daughter Angela? The doctor said she would call her." Pushing herself slowly up into a sitting position with her frail arms, she picked up a mirror from her bedside table. She scowled at the lined face with parched skin that stared back at her. "Is that really me? I look like a ghost," she said.

"Where's your hairbrush? I'll have you looking gorgeous again in no time. Although I'm sure your granddaughter doesn't care how you look," the nurse said.

Downstairs, Georgina devoured her egg and toast, surprised at how hungry she was; she didn't normally eat breakfast, and this was the second one she'd eaten in a day. She waited for a while, strangely anxious about her imminent reunion with a grandmother she hardly knew anymore. Georgina had never looked back at life in England after leaving Moreton College; like her mother, she found living in New York far more exciting than Worcester. But she hadn't understood the damage her parents' absence in her formative years had caused. Left to her own devices, she'd unconsciously wrapped her loneliness in a protective cocoon of self-interest, which until this moment had seemed quite normal. Somewhat alarmed, she realized she hadn't given her grandmother a moment's thought in many years.

Finally, she plucked up the courage to go upstairs, pulled her cardigan protectively around her waist, and knocked gently on the door.

Eve squinted at the tall, elegant young woman standing at the foot of her bed.

"Is that really you, Georgina?" she asked.

Eve felt her mind was playing games with her. The light catching Georgina's blue eyes and the highlights of her blonde hair made her look like someone else; someone from her past. She gasped.

"Goodness, it is you."

Georgina looked around the room, with its hospital bed and assorted medical paraphernalia, noticing that Eve's boney hands were trembling slightly. She didn't recognize the frail old lady with wispy white hair like spun sugar and skin as thin as tissue paper. It couldn't possibly be her grandmother; she had always been far more vital. Wind from the open window blew the curtains back and forth and a sensation of unexpected concern made her shiver involuntarily. Everything seemed to have shrunk—the street, the house, and now her Grandy. Confusion yielded to guilt for her years of selfishness, suddenly making her feel quite ashamed.

"May I sit on your bed?" Georgina gestured to the pink quilt counterpane. She took her grandmother's hand in hers and squeezed it gently. "I'm sorry you're not feeling well." Her throat felt inexplicably tight and she thought she might cry.

Eve reached out, touching her granddaughter on the cheek. "It does my heart good to see you." She brushed Georgina's hair away from her face with her sinewy hand and cupped her chin tenderly. "You were always such a pretty girl—just like your mother. Is she here too?"

"No, she's on a cruise in the Mediterranean. She should be back in a couple of weeks. She asked me to come and check on how you're getting on—I'm so sorry I haven't been to see you for such a long time."

Eve's hands were still trembling as she picked up the bone china cup and saucer from the tray on her bedside table. The cup jingled against the saucer as she raised it to her lips. "You're here now, that's all that matters. I'm so glad you came. Perhaps your mother will come when she's ready."

As tears started to prick her eyes, Georgina gave into the

disquieting and unfamiliar emotions that were forcing their way into her heart with unexpected urgency. She laid her head on Eve's pillow and sobbed like a child. She was completely bewildered. She didn't expect to feel this tug of familial love. Eve too was surprised that Georgina was so upset. She put her arms around her and kissed the top of her head. "You must be exhausted after your journey. A nice hot bath will soon have you feeling better. I'm sure Eileen will show you where everything is. We'll have plenty of time to catch up later."

Eileen led Georgina to the bathroom at the end of the landing, fetching a fresh white towel from the airing cupboard and a spare dressing-gown of Eve's. She handed them to Georgina.

"I'm glad you've come," she said. "You've given her a reason to keep going."

Stepping through the threshold, Georgina noticed with dismay that her grandmother's interior remodeling skills hadn't extended to the bathroom. The narrow bathtub had only a hand spray cradled in a rack over the taps, looking oddly like an old-fashioned telephone. She wondered how on earth she would survive these archaic conditions.

Yet as she turned on the tap, hot gushing water quickly filled the room with soothing steam. Blue bottles lined a shelf above the sink; opening one, she sniffed the rim before pouring the clear liquid into the bath. The water frothed with white bubbles, releasing a delicate perfume of roses. Tentatively she tested the water with her toe; after adding some more cold, she slowly lowered herself in.

Georgina couldn't remember when she had last taken a bath, but her grandmother was right: this was just what she needed.

Camilla shrieked when she saw Georgina striding towards her later that evening. She slid off the sleek leather dining chair, waving her hands in the air like a cheerleader. "This is lovely. Is it cashmere?" she asked, her cheek touching Georgina's soft cerise coat as she gave her a hug.

"Yes," Georgina replied. "You know me and pink. I couldn't resist it." She plonked herself down with an exaggerated thud across from her friend. "It's taken two days to get here. I wish I'd taken a nap this afternoon."

The pub in the center of Worcester where Camilla chose to meet up was well known for its gourmet meals and sophisticated clientele. Their table was next to an open kitchen, where the chef and his sous-chefs were busy concocting delicacies from locally sourced organic produce. The aroma in the room was mouthwatering; waiters in long black aprons darted back and forth, bearing small plates of complimentary *amuse-bouche* to stimulate their clients' appetites for the meal that was to follow.

"Would you like some?" Camilla pointed to a bottle of Prosecco sitting in an ice bucket next to the table. "I've finished almost half the bottle while I've been waiting and I'm starving. Although, the waiter did bring me these. I saved some for you." She picked up a plate of brioche toasts topped with whipped goat's cheese, slivers of beetroot, and microgreens. "They're so yummy—now tell me, how's your grandmother?"

Georgina took a deep slug of the chilled wine and popped a canape in her mouth. "Oh my God, I can't believe how old she is—I barely recognized her. It's upset me so much to see her—she's so tiny and weak. She's still with it though. Her nurse says that I've given her a reason to keep going. I'm so glad I came. But I can tell that she's disappointed Mum hasn't been to visit her."

"I remember your grandmother. She's such a sweet lady. I could never understand why she and your mother never got along. She reached over and squeezed Georgina's hand. "You look different. Your hair is longer, last time we Facetimed it was much shorter. I like it. I love your trousers too." Camilla, whose mother always referred to her daughter as "pleasantly plump," stared wistfully at Georgina's long legs encased in black leather. "I could never get away with those. I'd look like a baby elephant squeezed into a bin bag."

"Don't be silly. You could never look like an elephant. More like a cuddly teddy bear."

"Thanks a bunch! I'm not sure if that's a compliment or not. Anyway, I could never be a size zero like you, I like food too much."

"I didn't mean it like that. I could never be like you either. Kids and a career, you're amazing. You know me, I'd be a terrible wife and mother," Georgina said. There wasn't much they didn't know about each other. They'd become firm friends when they shared a dorm room at school. Back then no one could ever figure the unlikely pair out. Georgina, the extrovert, was always chasing boys and skipping classes, while Camilla was the more reserved and studious one. But she lived vicariously through Georgina. Not having to behave like her rebellious friend, but somehow experiencing the riskiness of Georgina's life, was exhilarating. And Georgina loved the security that Camilla gave her. Camilla was very protective of her wayward friend. When Georgina's father announced he was divorcing her mother, Camilla was the one who crawled into bed with her. She'd hugged her sleepless friend tight, trying to take away some of the pain she was feeling.

"So, how's the new job going?" Georgina asked.

"I'm lucky they let me work from home. Remember how awful it was for me when Henry was a toddler? I never seemed to be at home, and I missed out on such a lot. The nanny got to hear his first word, saw him walk for the first time. It was a ghastly time if I'm honest. I don't want to miss anything with Daisy. We've got an *au-pair* now who's wonderful."

"That sounds like a perfect solution. I can't even imagine

how you do it all."

"It's great—you should try it one day. By the way, where's your mother off to this time?" Camilla put down the dinner menu and beckoned a waiter to come over to take their order.

"It's one of those singles cruises to Greece, I think."

"Oh my God. You know that there's an epidemic of STDs among wrinklies going on cruises. I hope your mother is being careful."

"Did you have to share that with me?" Georgina squeezed her eyes shut and gave a fake shudder. Just then her phone beeped. "Oh no! I could be in the Hamptons right now with Josh Bankcroft. He's just split up with his girlfriend. I've wanted to shag Josh for ages, but he always has someone in tow."

Camilla frowned. She ran her hands through her wavy brown hair in exasperation. Before she could stop herself, words came blurting out of her mouth. "Honestly Georgie, you can't mean that. Do you still sleep around like you did in your twenties? You don't want to end up like your mother."

Georgina felt her face turn hot, surprised by Camilla's words. "Do you really think I'm like my mum?"

"She only thinks about herself." She stopped abruptly. "My bad. Sorry, it's none of my business. What are you going to have to eat?"

Georgina bit her lip to stop herself from crying. It stung her to think that Camilla thought badly of her. "I can't believe you think I'm selfish like my mother. You've never said anything like that before," she said.

"I didn't exactly say that. I said you might turn out like her. I never said you're selfish. Do you think the pasta is gluten-free?" she asked while flicking through the menu.

The waiter, who was hovering near their table, shook his head.

"I'm afraid we don't have gluten-free pasta on the menu, madam," he said. "The special today is a Dover sole, caught off the coast of Cornwall, served on the bone with locally grown asparagus and Jersey Royal potatoes. If you would prefer, the chef will fillet the fish for you."

Taking another look at the menu, Georgina forced herself to smile at the waiter before handing it back to him. "The special sounds perfect. Off the bone. No potatoes though. Perhaps the chef could steam me some spinach instead of the asparagus, and absolutely no butter on anything. No garlic either. Oh, and the wine list, too," Georgina said.

"You're turning all New York on me. No wonder you're skinnier than ever. No this, no that! And what's wrong with asparagus?"

"It makes your wee smell awful. Didn't you know that?" Georgina snapped back.

Camilla raised her eyebrows and handed the waiter her menu. "I'll have the Dover sole, off the bone too please. But I'm happy with however it's prepared. Thank you." She took a large swig of her wine. "So, what are your plans?" she asked, completely unaware that her friend was looking a little peeved.

Georgina carried on, trying to put Camilla's words out of her mind. "Well, Eileen who's looking after Grandy seems nice. She's made a bed up for me in the box room, but it's cramped, and you should see the bathroom. No shower—it's awful. I was wondering if I could come to stay with you and Matt."

"I don't think that's a good idea. Matt's grandfather had a caregiver living with him before he died. One day we discovered bruises all over his body. You need to stay there and keep an eye on things."

"That's terrible." Georgina winced. "I can't see Eileen ever hurting Grandy though. She really seems to care about her. Gosh, I don't seem to get anything right, do I? I feel dreadful that I haven't seen more of her over the years."

"I'm sure she must be happy you're here—I am too. I hope

we can get to see more of each other—we've been drifting apart. Let me know if Matt and I can do anything to help. Now, tell me—what's going on with you these days?"

"Apart from being a thoughtless granddaughter who sleeps around, eats nothing, and is selfish, you mean?" Georgina stuck out her tongue. "You're beginning to sound like the mother I never had. Why are you being so snippy?"

"I'm sorry, I should have kept my big mouth shut. Maybe it could have something to do with the half bottle of Prosecco I've just necked. Can we start over?"

Georgina nodded.

Camilla looked relieved. "How's that new app for the online auction coming?"

"Well, that never got off the ground. But I've a new project in the works. I helped organize a fundraiser for a children's charity last month too. We had a fun run in Central Park and a masked ball at The Pierre Hotel. It went really well," she said.

"Very impressive. Did you run?"

"Yes—well, I walked the last mile. I worked with the loveliest old couple to organize the ball; we made lots of money."

"What's the new project?"

"I'm making a facial scrub. You remember I told you about the one that I discovered when I went to Peru? It's made with quinoa, honey, and apricot seeds."

"I think so," Camilla said.

"Well, I've managed to get hooked up with my friend Jen's cosmetics company that donates part of their profits to environmental and social causes. Now we have to figure out the production. I've never done anything like this before, but luckily I've some contacts who can help me out."

"That's amazing! I love the philanthropic and environmental aspects of it. Who's Jen?"

"I only met her last year..."

Two waiters interrupted their conversation, simultaneously

placing their plates down in front of them with a theatrical flourish.

"Truce?" Camilla asked sheepishly. "I'm sorry for being so grouchy and judgmental."

Georgina reached out and touched her hand. "That's alright. You're still my BFF. Even if you have had some sort of personality transplant!"

The next morning Georgina was having breakfast when Eileen came downstairs.

"Your grandmother would like to see you," she said. "She had a restless night, but she's anxious to talk to you."

Georgina finished her tea and toast, and leaving her dirty dishes on the table, she headed upstairs to see Eve.

"Have you heard from your mother yet?" Eileen called after her.

"No. She hasn't returned my calls. I've texted her so many times, but nothing. I've decided to stay until she gets back."

Eve's eyes were closed when Georgina opened the door to her bedroom. She shut it quietly behind her and went over to sit on the chair next to her bed. The old lady's eyes flickered open. "There you are, dear. Did you have a nice time with your friend last night?" She coughed and fumbled for her oxygen mask. She took a couple of deep breaths before letting the mask drop down onto her chest.

"Yes, it was lovely to see her again. How are you feeling today?"

"Much the same as I do most days. But I have so much to tell you before you leave," she fretted, her hands gripping the bedsheets.

"Don't worry. I'm not going anywhere for a while," Georgina said, reaching for her grandmother's hand and stroking it. "I definitely won't leave until Mum arrives."

"That's a lot to ask of a busy young thing like you."

"Work can wait. You told me yesterday that you have something very important to share with us. Is it something that you can tell me before Mum gets here?"

Eve's eyes flashed at the open window and then back to look at Georgina as if she was fearful of something.

"You know, you have your grandfather's eyes."

"My grandfather?" Georgina looked surprised. "No one has ever told me anything about him."

"He keeps coming to me in my dreams and here you are looking just like him. I don't have very long left, dear. You need to hear my story before it's too late. It's time to break my silence."

CHAPTER 3

EVE

Worcester, England, 1943

The glove shop in Friars Lane above which Eve Harrison grew up had been in the family for over a century. To the left of the front door, one large picture window displayed both men's and women's gloves on stands of varying heights. A black shop sign over the door read in gilt lettering: "*SIDNEY HARRISON & SON – GLOVEMAKERS EST.1802.*"

Before the War, Friars Lane was a bustling commercial street. Mrs. Gould next door ran the stationery shop, where locals could get their pens and ink, blotting paper and note-paper. At the beginning of the school year children would queue up to buy their geometric compasses, set squares, and books of logarithm tables. Still to this day, Eve associated old Mrs. Gould's vinegary meanness with going back to school.

Luckily Mr. Talbot in the bookshop was much more fun. He didn't care how much time Eve and her friends spent browsing through picture books or encyclopedias. He'd in-herited the shop after his father died, but he always wanted to be a teacher, not a bookshop owner. He'd pull up a chair and read aloud to his young customers—chapters from *Treasure Island*, *Swallows and Amazons*, or Eve's favorite, *The Secret Garden*. She still had echoes in her mind of his voice bringing the stories to life.

Then there was the haberdasher a few doors further up the street: Eve remembered the times, when, as a little girl digging through the drawers of sparkly buttons, she imagined she was a treasure hunter searching for rare jewels, while her mother dithered over the perfect fabric from the rolls of gingham, linen, silks, and heavy tweeds.

At *Harrison's,* Eve's parents carried on the family business, crafting "made to measure" gloves for the wealthy of Worcester, as well as more affordable and serviceable ones for daily use. Eve grew up with the smell of leather in her nostrils and the whirring sound of the sewing machine in her ears; she learned the craft almost by osmosis. But as the War started, Eve dreamed of doing more with her life—even before tragedy struck Worcester.

The day of the bombing was stamped on her brain. It was 1940 when a lone Junkers 88 dropped a bomb on a factory not far from her school. The children were having lunch in the school cafeteria when they heard an enormous explosion. Rushing out, she caught sight of the airplane flying overhead, its big black swastikas clearly visible. Six people working in the factory that made parts for barrage balloons were killed, and many more were injured. Even though she was only fifteen, she'd immediately registered for the St. John's Ambulance course, with visions of being a front-line nurse, saving lives while dressed in a crisp white uniform.

War changed Friars Lane. Mr. Talbot closed his shop when he was called up to serve, and the haberdasher's supplies had dwindled, causing her to open for half days only. The busiest shops were on the other side of town: the butchers, bakers, and grocers where housewives spent many long hours with their ration cards in hand, queuing to get what little food was allotted to them.

Customers weren't buying new gloves at *Harrison's,* but they were bringing in their old ones to be fixed, supporting the government's "Make Do and Mend" initiative. The armed forces became the family's biggest client: Eve's parents opened a new factory space where they worked at full capacity.

"Dad, I want to talk to you about something," Eve said one evening before supper.

Outside, the sun was starting to fall behind the roofs of the houses opposite. A soft glow of light warmed the faded upholstery of the family's three-piece suite in the living room above the shop, glimmering on the peeling wallpaper and making the space seem cozier than it really was. There was an aroma of cooking coming from the kitchen, and under the window a small dining table with four chairs was set for the evening meal.

"What's that, love?" Ernest said from behind his newspaper. A lit pipe burned in the ashtray on a table next to his chair. He reached for it and took a puff. "I hope you don't have bad news for me. I've had a long day at the factory trying to get out this latest order for the RAF, and City have lost again." He tossed the paper on the floor. "All our best players have signed up."

Eve shivered and bent down to switch on the new electric fire which sat proudly in the old fireplace. The two bars feebly glowed red and crackled as the heat burned off the surface dust. She was wearing a deep blue sweater that her mother had re-knit using the yarn from an old cardigan of her father's. Her mother had suggested adding mother-of-pearl buttons which changed it from a plain old jumper into a chic tailored top. Clothing coupons didn't stretch that far, so she was lucky that her mum was handy with a needle.

"Is that a new jumper?" he asked. "I've never seen it before."

Eve giggled. Her bobbed hair shone like chestnuts, and she flicked it in the air as she did a twirl to show off her new sweater. "No, it used to be your cardigan—Mum's brilliant at knitting."

"Hells bells! I'm not going to have any clothes left the way you two are carrying on. I saw her eyeing up my dressing gown the other day. You and your mum's fancy fashion ideas." He chuckled to himself before noticing that his daughter's hazel eyes had turned serious. "Well, spit it out—what have you got to tell me?"

She tilted her head to one side and blurted out, "I'm going to train to be a nurse. I went to the flicks the other night and saw the Newsreel about Dunkirk—they were asking for nurses to sign up. I've done my St. John's Ambulance course and they said that should count towards my training. I signed up yesterday. I start next week—but I really want your blessing."

Ernest scowled. "Oh, Evie, I don't want to think of you in the middle of all that fighting. You're my little girl. You're doing such a valuable job here helping with the war effort. But I suppose I don't have an objection to you training to become a nurse."

Eve climbed on his lap and wrapped her arms around his neck. She could usually get her way with her father, but she knew that, for him, this was a huge concession. She kissed his whiskery cheek. His gray hair was thinning, his eyes hooded with age. For the first time in her life, she realized that he was getting old. She wasn't his little girl any longer; it was time to follow her dreams.

"Thank you, Daddy. It's what I really, really want to do. I want to help, and I know I'll be good at it—and guess what? Maybe I'll be able to look after you when you've got one foot in the grave."

"Crikey—I don't know if I like the sound of that. I haven't forgotten you kept tying me up in bandages when you did that ambulance course. I looked like a mummy."

He kissed her forehead.

"Perhaps the war will be over before you finish training, and they won't have to send you off to some distant land," he said. "You're growing up far too quickly for my liking. We'll still need you in the shop sometimes, though. Maybe you can help train a new girl to do the repair work. The factory is taking up all my time and your mum's too. Did she tell you that the latest batch of pigskin is useless? We're supposed to be making gloves for the Army with it. Something must have gone wrong with the tanning process. It'll take hours longer than usual to make it work. It's never-ending..."

Véronique, Eve's mother, was listening quietly to their conversation from the other side of the kitchen door. Her red painted fingernails nervously fluttered over her apron. She didn't want her daughter going off to war any more than her husband. But Eve could be very headstrong and telling her no sometimes made her even more so. She flung the door open. "*Mon Dieu*! Enough with your grumbling, Ernie. Things aren't that bad. Maybe it'll be a good thing if Eve is a nurse—she can look after you when you're a grumpy old man and I won't have to."

"Not bad?" he exclaimed. "You weren't there when that idiot from the Ministry of Defense came in to ask if we could modify the flight gloves for the RAF—as if I haven't got enough to do. Now I must come up with a pattern to install a zipper to make them easier to put on and off...You're right: maybe she should get that nursing training finished quick. The way I'm working, I'm going to be an old man sooner than you both think."

"*Mais alors, tu es déjà un vieil homme et aussi un grincheux.* You know you love a good challenge—and you always enjoy telling us all how clever you are when you succeed."

Ernest turned to Eve and frowned.

"*Maman* said you're already an old man and a grumpy one too," Eve translated for him.

Véronique grinned and turned to her daughter. "Go find Frankie for me, *ma chérie.* Dinner's ready—tell him it's his favorite. *Ce soir, c'est une délicieuse soupe de pommes de terres avec des orties,*" she said, pressing her thumb and first finger to her lips, making a loud kissing sound.

"You can insult me all you want in that fancy language of yours. I recognize that bloody potato and nettle soup when I hear it, though, and I can smell it too." Ernest laughed. "I've got your number, Frenchie, even if I'm the luckiest man alive with the two prettiest girls to prove it. I suppose I'll just have to suffer the soup again."

"It's good for you. The recipe in The Ministry of Food pamphlet says that nettles are full of protein and iron, and I got some nasty stings picking them. It's not just your heart I care about, *mon amour.*"

Ernest was always in awe of his wife's resourcefulness at creating meals out of nothing, but this soup was not his favorite. The previous week she managed to get a piece of oxtail at the butcher's. There was precious little meat on the tail bone, but the stew she made, bulked out with carrots and parsnips grown in their back garden, was delicious. As the War progressed and rationing took over, Ernest dug up all Véronique's flower gardens, replacing them with row upon row of vegetables. Now, as well as the vegetables they grew, they stretched out their food allowance with greens, like nettles and dandelion leaves, and mushrooms and berries foraged in the fields and hedgerows.

Véronique giggled girlishly and whacked him over the

head with a tea towel as he tried to pull her onto his knee. "Let me go, you, old grouch, you! Mrs. Smith gave me some of her Bramleys, so there's baked apples and that terrible English custard you love *pour le désert*." She pecked him on the cheek.

"Do you lovebirds ever stop bickering? You're like a couple of squabbling chickens." Eve grinned at her crazy parents. However much they bickered, she knew that love was always in the air. She loved their romantic story about meeting at an artisan fair in Paris. Véronique Dupuis was visiting the capital from Grenoble, where she worked in her family's glove-making business, and Ernest Harrison was with a group of glovemakers from Worcester. It was love at first sight, or *un coup de foudre*, as she called it. Her family was astonished when she followed *"un Rosbif"* back to the land of watery stews and overcooked vegetables.

Véronique and Ernest had always wanted another child after Eve, but it never happened. So, they couldn't have been more delighted when Frankie arrived in their lives two years earlier. Frank Boxer was a cheeky evacuee from London. His nose was splashed with orangey-brown freckles to match his hair, and he had a gap between his two front teeth. During the War, every household with a spare bedroom had been required to take in a child from the city, where the relentless Nazi bombing was making life dangerous. Children were relocated to the relative safety of the countryside far from their homes. Most of them were desperately unhappy to be separated from their families, and some only stayed for a brief time, but Frank was one of the lucky ones. The Harrison family welcomed him with open arms. Eve teased him mercilessly but playfully, imitating his cockney accent, while he mimicked the French manner-isms she'd inherited from her mother. She taught him French words which he surprised her by picking up very quickly.

Frank adored *"ma soeur,"* as he learned to call her. Eve won him over with her warm smile and her sense of fun, telling him jokes and playing card games. As her parents were busy managing the factory, they were thrilled that Eve, then seventeen, took the little lodger under her wing.

One day shortly after he first arrived, Frank came home with a black eye, skinned knees, and a tear-stained face. At ten, he was small for his age, making him fair game for older boys.

"What's happened, Frankie? Are you alright?" Eve asked.

"Nothing. I've got some homework to do." He shrugged, avoiding her eyes, making for the safety of his bedroom.

"Well, you don't look like nothing's happened, so spill the beans." Eve took a sugary pear drop out of a white paper bag and gave it to him.

"I was playing 'conkers' with me mates. Some boys from the big school tried to take them off us. When we said no, they gave us a right pummeling."

Eve was horrified. "Can you tell me who they are?"

"I'm no snitch. I'm not telling you." He sucked on the pear drop defiantly.

"I understand why you're scared," Eve said, "but I'm going to find out somehow. I don't like bullies and they're not going to get away with it if I have anything to do with it. Come on—let's get you cleaned up before *Maman* comes home."

The following week she hatched a plan to watch Frank and his friends after school. The playground, at the back of the school, was out of sight of passersby. Eve hid behind a tree to wait while Frank happily played with some of the other evacuees in town. After a few minutes, a group of tall, lanky teenagers approached the children. One of the boys grabbed Frank by the collar, shouting at him to hand over his playthings. He shook him several times before throwing him to the ground, then he grabbed Frank's catapult out of his hand. Just as he was about to load it up, Eve sprang into action.

"Hey! What do you think you're doing?" she yelled. The

anger that had been simmering inside for several days now reached a boiling point. The older boys turned around and scoffed, laughing at the girl running towards them.

A greasy-haired lad swaggered towards her, hands in his pockets, shirt hanging out, and bony knees protruding through torn trousers

"Well, look who we have here—it's little Miss Fixit, innit? Clear off and mind your own business." His face was dotted with angry-looking pimples. Eve laughed quietly to herself. She thought it was funny that his teeth looked like a rat's; with his high-pitched voice, he sounded like one too.

"It is my business. That's my brother you're manhandling. You touch him again and you'll have me to deal with. You don't scare me."

"Don't make me laugh—you couldn't take the skin off a rice pudding. He's not your brother, he's one of them evacuees from London." He spat on the ground, wiping his mouth on his sleeve.

As she turned to look at Frank, the boy came behind her and grabbed her arm. Feeling his steamy breath on her hair, she caught hold of him by his other wrist, pulling him closer. With the heel of the shoe on her right foot, she scraped his shinbone as hard as she could. He quickly fell to the ground squealing in pain. "What did you do that for?" he yelped, reaching down to rub his leg.

"You come near Frank or me again and I'll do worse—you bully."

He was shocked that she had the better of him; he hadn't expected the little grasshopper to be such a force to be reckoned with.

A lone figure stood outside the shop door. He peered in through the window, seeming to hesitate before pressing the

latch. The bell above the door rattled loudly. Eve looked up, startled. Customers had stopped coming at the end of the day, now that all the other shops were closed early. He didn't look like one of her regular customers. As he came closer, she noticed that his uniform displayed the rank of Wing Commander. He loomed over her, rubbing his moustache, bowing his shoulders slightly as he spoke to her.

"Good evening—I hope I've come to the right place." He removed his gloves and put them on the long wooden counter. "I'm looking for Eve Harrison."

"That's me, "Eve said. "If you need those repaired quickly, I won't be able to get to them until next week."

It was getting dark outside in the street; the light from the single electric light bulb glowed weakly from the ceiling, casting ominous shadows in the corners of the shop. Eve pulled her cardigan protectively around her waist.

The man picked up his gloves and put them in his pocket. "No, no. They're in perfectly good condition, thank you. Actually, I'm hoping that you'll be able to help me."

Eve frowned. She turned to look at the door behind her. "My Dad should be down in a minute, maybe he can help," she lied. She swallowed nervously; her parents were both at the factory on the other side of town.

"No, it's you I need to speak to, and it's a matter of the highest secrecy."

"I'm not sure how I can help you." Eve pulled a face.

"There's nothing to worry about, I can assure you," the man said. "I am Wing Commander Ray Drummond. I've come to enlist your services in the war effort. I believe you're a fluent French speaker and that your mother's family are also glovemakers in France."

"How do you know about *Maman's* family? You're right, I am fluent—my mother is from Grenoble. She always talks to me in French. We don't speak it around my dad, though. It makes him cross when he can't understand what we're saying."

Drummond laughed. "I can remember my father feeling the same way. My mother is French, too."

"*Maman* had news last year from my uncle to say that my cousin has gone into hiding because *les Allemandes* wanted to send him to work in a factory in Germany. It sounds awful. We've heard nothing from *Tonton* for months now."

"Because of your special skills, I would like you to come to RAF Pershore with me to discuss what we have in mind. I'm hoping we can rely on you to help your country."

"Of course," Eve's face flushed pink with excitement. "How did you know that I am going to be a nurse? I only signed up the other day."

"I'll send a car to pick you up tomorrow," Drummond said with the authority of a man who is used to being obeyed.

CHAPTER 4

GEORGINA AND EVE
Worcester, England, 2016

The chirruping of garden birds trickled down from the rooftops. Georgina and Eileen managed to help Eve out to a stone terrace at the back of the house, where grandmother and granddaughter sat underneath an apple tree, its branches tinged with pale pink blossoms. A look of calm satisfaction came over Eve as she settled into her chair and gazed at her work. After retiring in her late fifties, she'd broadened her interests to include gardening, and the flowers surrounding them were a tribute to her passion. By now, the early spring snowdrops and crocuses had died off, giving way to deep blue irises and yellow daffodils; while clusters of soft pink tulips nodded their heads in the breeze, nestling next to clumps of bright green hostas. A variety of evergreen and deciduous shrubs composed the foundation plantings of the curved beds, bordering a neatly trimmed lawn the size of a large pocket-handkerchief. Eve's favorite climbing rose, which bloomed deep pink in the summer and again in the autumn, covered the wall closest to the house. She was proud to have built such a haven in the center of town; hidden behind high stone walls, with a wooden gate leading to a back alleyway, it was her own secret garden.

Sailing clouds were blocking the sun, adding a chill to the strengthening breeze. Georgina tucked a thick tartan blanket around her grandmother's knees before picking up her phone again to look at her messages.

"Can't you put that thing down for a moment, dear? You're always looking at it," Eve said.

Georgina shoved her phone in her pocket. "Well, my friends have forgotten all about me anyway. I don't know why I bother," she said with an edge to her voice.

"Anyone special you're fretting over?" Eve asked, picking up on her granddaughter's mood.

"I'm not fretting, but yes, there is someone. Or there was. He's not right for me though."

"What do you mean 'not right'?"

"My friend Scarlett thinks he's probably after my money."

"Do you think that he is?"

"How can I be sure he isn't?"

"I can't tell you that. All I know is, you'll know when you've found the right one."

"Oh Gran, I don't want to marry anyone. I was just having fun with Marco. I don't love him. He was great in the bedroom, though." She blushed. "Sorry! I can't believe I just told you that."

"Don't worry, you can't shock me—we old things know what sex is."

Georgina reached into her pocket for her phone. "That's him, Grandy," she said.

Eve peered at the screen and smiled. "Very handsome. He looks like an actor I saw on the telly. What does your mother say about him?"

"Oh goodness—I haven't told her about him. She's never

been interested in my boyfriends. And knowing her, she'd be horrified that he's a waiter."

"Yes, your mother has always been a dreadful snob."

"Why am I so confused? I thought by my age I was supposed to know what I'm doing."

"Life doesn't always follow the path you think it will, dear," Eve said quietly.

Eileen came out with a tray of tea and biscuits and put it on the wrought iron table. Pouring milk and then tea into two china teacups, Georgina gave one to her grandmother. Eve took a sip and grimaced.

"You keep forgetting I like two sugars in my tea, dear." Eve handed Georgina back the cup.

"That's an awful lot of sugar, Grandy—you know it's bad for your heart, don't you?"

There was a playful smirk on Eve's lips. "Is it really? How did I ever make it to ninety-three, then? We're all going to die of something. I'm going to enjoy my tea until I do, so mind your own business!"

Georgina felt a laugh tickle her throat.

"You go, girl!" she said.

"We didn't have much sugar during the War, you know. *Maman* told us if we didn't have it in our tea, she could save it to make more cakes. I don't remember her making many cakes though—we didn't have enough butter...."

Once the tea was sweetened to her taste, Eve picked up a gingersnap, dunking it defiantly in the china cup. Georgina burst out laughing. She admired her grandmother's feistiness, even if she disapproved of her sweet tooth.

"Did you always work in the shop and sell gloves when you were young?" Georgina asked.

"Yes, I sold gloves and I repaired them too, but I was a glovemaker by trade. In those days you did what you were told."

"Mum always told me the shop was an awful place."

"Your mother was never a happy child. But I blame myself for some of that. When I came back from France at the end of the War, I found out I was pregnant. My parents told me I needed to find a father for her. I knew they were ashamed. I married in the rush to give her a name and to make them happy. I never loved him. Tom was a bully who made our lives a misery. I didn't discover until later that he was unkind to Angela. She's never forgiven me."

"You're kidding. I never knew any of this. Mum never told me you were divorced. When I think about it, I don't think she's ever mentioned her father either. Did you ever tell Mum who her real father is?"

"No, I couldn't tell anyone. It's a part of my life I've locked away for an awfully long time. Losing him broke my heart into pieces. I shut myself off to the idea of ever loving again. I wasn't the best mother, I know, but I did the best I could."

"I'm sure you did." Georgina squeezed her grandmother's hand.

"Angela was always so difficult. She was a bolshie teenager, she always liked to pretend she was someone she wasn't. She refused to help in the shop—said it was beneath her." She paused for a moment to take a sip of tea.

Eve pushed her dark sunglasses back on her head, at the same time frowning, as if the action would somehow help her to fathom what her grandmother was telling her. There were so many twists and turns.

"Was Frank still living here when you got back?"

"No, he'd moved back to London by then and was mixing with some bad-uns. But he came for the wedding. That day he and Tom had the most awful fight, real fisty-cuff stuff. Tom came up the aisle with a huge shiner. Frank went back to London and I never saw him again. To this day I have no idea what it was about. It's all such a long time ago. I sometimes wonder what became of him."

"I would have liked a brother or sister. I don't really think of Ben as a sibling. He's so much younger than me."

"As families go, we're a bit of a mess, aren't we? I suppose I wasn't a good grandmother either, was I?"

"I can't believe I never questioned why I hardly ever saw you. I was a pretty awful granddaughter."

Georgina's mind was still whirring with what her grandmother had told her about her ex-husband. Her mother's childhood sounded far from happy. Some of what Eve told her did help to explain Angela's selfishness and lack of warmth. "When you said Tom was unkind to Mum, are you saying he was abusive?"

"I don't think he hurt her, but he was verbally abusive. He was a bad drunk who spent most of the days in the pub when he could. When he came home, Angela of course witnessed his nasty moods. I did my best to protect her. My parents weren't surprised when I divorced him, but I knew I'd let them down. In those days I'd committed two sins—getting pregnant out of wedlock and getting divorced."

"People don't think like that now. Didn't Mum have any friends? I don't think I could have survived without Camilla."

"No, I don't think she did. Well, she never bought anyone home that I remember. We lived upstairs over the shop. She complained it was a shabby place—I suppose it was if I'm honest. She was always ashamed of where she lived. I'd hoped, with Tom gone, things would be better. But she couldn't wait to leave home. Luckily for her she was a resourceful girl. She'd learned French from me and my mother when she was little. Then she found a job in London. I never saw her much after that—I hoped that when she married your father, she'd be happy...but money doesn't buy you happiness, does it?"

Georgina considered everything her grandmother had told her—the War, returning home pregnant, her mother's unhappiness. Wary of pushing her fragile grandmother too far, she again changed the subject.

"Is glove-making difficult to do?"

"I wouldn't say it's hard, but it is a learned skill. Nowadays, of course, most of the work is done by machine. In my day there were sewing machines, but a lot of the work was done by hand. Every animal skin is different and learning how to stretch the leather to get the right amount of give requires a special talent. I also learned how to cut to a pattern, to shape, and to stitch the gloves."

"Gosh—that must have been very time-consuming. You couldn't make very many in a week if you did most of it by hand, could you?"

"No dear, that's true. Gloves were sent out to women who would do the hand stitching in their own homes. It was called 'piecework.' The gloves were stitched inside out and then turned and stretched on a glove form. Then all the wrinkles and grooves were ironed out. When I went to France under-cover, it was my job to take the unfinished gloves to workers in the outlying areas. That's how I established contact with other agents."

"Are you serious? What do you mean you went to France 'undercover'? Were you a spy? I assumed you'd been visiting your mother's family when you mentioned France." Georgina raised her eyebrows. The pieces of the jigsaw puzzle that her grandmother had been laying down were starting to take shape.

"More of an undercover agent. It was all top secret. I worked as a courier and a radio operator. I helped transmit messages to England. I signed the Official Secrets Act. I've never told anyone about it until now."

"Hang on a minute. I thought you said you became a nurse."

"No, that was my plan. When Drummond's car arrived to pick me up, I thought it was to take me to nursing school, but instead we went to London. It wasn't until I arrived at the Special Operations Executive's office in Baker Street that I quickly realized he had other plans in mind. Before I knew it,

I found myself in front of a Selection Board of psychologists. The SOE recruited me because of my knowledge of French and my glove-making skills to become a secret agent in France. They sent me to work for my uncle in Grenoble while helping the Resistance. I still told my family I was becoming a nurse. But it was a lie."

"That's just unreal. You went to France as an 'agent'? It sounds like something out of a movie. I can't wait to hear more about that."

"I was excited about going. But it didn't turn out how I expected it to. *Maman* lost her entire family in France, but I couldn't tell her anything. I wrote letters home pretending I was still in England when I wasn't. It was hard, but I believed I was doing the right thing. I was a hero, or so they said." Eve trailed off, looking into the distance.

They sat in silence for a few minutes as Georgina held her grandmother's hand. She was beginning to understand the weighty significance of Eve's memories and the consequential impact on her life.

"You don't have to talk about it if it's making you too sad," she said.

After a while Eve seemed to regain her composure. "Would you like to see some of the gloves I made?"

"I'd love to. Do you still have them?"

"I have a box of them somewhere in my wardrobe. It's where I keep some of the kid gloves that I made for myself. The kidskin came from wild goats in the Alps. It's incredibly soft but it's the most pliable and resilient skin to work with."

"I have some pink Gucci gloves that I bought last year. They're kidskin and they cost a fortune, but I had to have them—pink's my favorite color."

"That's a coincidence dear—I love pink too. I also thought pink gloves were the height of elegance when I was young."

Georgina had never drawn the connection between her obsession for gloves and her grandmother's trade. She decided that there must be some weird genetic link.

"Fancy us both having the same favorite color, too. I must have inherited your sense of style."

"Well, I wasn't always an old lady, you know. I was quite the fashionista when I was young."

"Well, I think you've definitely still got it."

"Thank you, dear." Eve touched her wispy white hair. "I used to have such thick hair when I was young. *'La couleur des châtaignes'* — 'the color of chestnuts', *Maman* used to say."

"I wish Mum had taught me French when I was little," Georgina said wistfully. "She never taught me anything."

"You were such a stubborn little girl. Even if she had tried to teach you, you probably would have refused! But it's never too late to learn."

As they chatted on, the sky became gloomy, the day slowly fading, and the dampening air produced an earthy smell in the garden. A few fat raindrops plopped onto the metal garden table at the same time as the wind picked up. Eve pulled her cardigan around her shoulders. Georgina touched her grand-mother's hand. "Oh goodness, you're freezing. Let's get you inside. I have some work emails to answer, but after that I'll go on a glove hunt."

Later that evening, Georgina found a tower of shoe boxes stacked on top of each other on the floor of the walnut-paneled wardrobe. There were several that looked as if they hadn't been touched for years. A strong smell of mothballs made her sneeze. She glanced over to check she hadn't disturbed Eve.

Quietly she examined each one until found the one her grandmother had spoken of. Stamped on the lid in gold were the words: "*Magasin de Chaussures Pierre Lacroix, 21 rue de la Rose, Grenoble, 38.*" Her fingers skimmed over the em-bossed letters, wiping away a layer of dust. She carefully opened the box to discover, covered by a layer of yellowing tissue paper, the most exquisite glove she had ever seen. The flawless leather was dyed a very pale pink. The lining of the glove was of soft cashmere wool, the wrist delicately scalloped, with edging accentuated by intricate stitching in a darker shade of pink and finished with pearl buttons. She gasped. She thought her expensive gloves were perfection, until she touched her grandmother's handiwork. As she lifted the glove out of the box, a faint hint of perfume tickled her nose.

Just as she was reaching into the box to look for the matching glove, she felt her phone vibrate. She pulled it out of her pocket, tiptoeing out onto the landing. She closed the door behind her.

"Is that you, Georgie?" Angela was shouting. Georgina held the phone away from her ear.

"Where are you? I thought you'd be here by now."

"Well, here's the thing, darling. Martin, a man I've met on the cruise, has had a bit of a mishap, so we're not able to fly home just yet. In fact, he's in hospital in Athens..."

"What do you mean a mishap? What's happened?"

"He's got a problem with his heart, but I can't really get into details on the phone. I won't be able to get to Worcester for a while, I'm afraid."

"That's marvelous," Georgina said sarcastically. "Grandy's been asking for you."

"I'm sorry, but I can't leave him now. What was that?... Georgina... I must go. There's a doctor who needs to talk to me..."

"Mum, wait... you need to get back here... Grandy wants to see you. She needs you. I need you..." She kept yelling into the phone as it went dead.

She crept back into Eve's bedroom, resisting the urge to scream at the top of her voice. Eve rested peacefully on her pillow, her hair puffed like a cloud, and dressed in her white nightgown, she looked almost ghostlike. Something about her stillness made Georgina's jaw stiffen and catch her breath. Her heart squeezed tightly. Not wanting to wake her, but terrified that her grandmother had stopped breathing, she tentatively touched her arm, willing her to move just a little. Then she noticed that Eve's eyes were quivering under her closed eyelids. Relieved, Georgina shivered, now fully grasping the fragile situation she was in. She didn't want her grandmother to die when they had just started to get to know each other. Eve was whispering softly in her sleep, her mouth twitching rapidly. Georgina kissed her on the forehead, tenderly straightening the rumpled bedsheets as if she was tucking up a small child for the night. She sat by Eve's bedside, protectively watching over her until she woke up.

"Is this what you've been looking for?" she asked when Eve opened her eyes.

Eve lifted herself up on one elbow. She had been having the nightmare again, the one where Frank lay dead on the ground, and she was frozen to the spot, unable to help him. By force of habit, she stiffened her back, smiling brightly. The box sat in front of her. She put on her reading glasses to check the label. "Oh, my goodness, this is it. This shoebox was from Monsieur Lacroix's shop. He was one of my contacts in the Resistance network. If he had a message to pass on, he would put a pair of red shoes in his window display. I passed by his shoe shop in rue de la Rose every other day to check—I've just remembered that."

"No way, Grandy! You had quite the adventure."

"He also sold expensive gloves. I made some special ones for him. Because I did such a decent job, he gave me the most beautiful pair of pink satin shoes that I had fallen in love with. He was a lovely old man."

Her head fell back onto the pillows.

Georgina marveled at her grandmother's experiences as she placed the box on the bed. Eve touched it, running her fingers over the lid, staring vacantly as if her mind had wandered elsewhere. After a while, she opened it and took out the pink glove.

"I made a pair for myself, too, thinking I would wear them

when I got married one day. They matched the pink shoes perfectly." She held the glove tenderly against her cheek.

"I was wondering if it was special. It's exquisite. But what happened to the other one? Did you wear them when you married that horrid man?"

"I could never find it, but even if I had, I would never have worn them when I married him. They're a memory of someone I hold very dear to my heart." She rummaged around in the box. As she delved, it slid slowly off the bed, landing on the floor with a thump.

"What's this, Grandy?" Georgina picked something shaped like a hand off the floor.

"That's a glove form. I used this one to hide my messages in."

"What messages?"

"The dispatches that we sent to England. Sometimes there were detailed instructions about German troop movements or requests for special equipment that couldn't be left to memory. Those needed to be transcribed accurately."

Georgina turned the metal object over to look at it in more detail. It was smooth and shiny, about the size and shape of a woman's hand and wrist. Deep inside one of the hollow fingers, she thought she saw something. "Is this one?" She carefully pulled out a note. The crispy paper crackled as she unfolded the long-lost communication.

Eve gulped nervously, her eyes darting from the glove form to the note in confusion. Georgina handed her the yellowing scrap of paper. She tentatively reached out to take it with a terrified look in her eyes. She looked at it for several minutes. Then her face changed to an expression of overwhelming sadness, as tears flowed unchecked down her cheeks.

CHAPTER 5

EVE AND SYLVIE
Scotland, 1943

The train chugged over the border into Scotland, where it stopped at the village of Gretna Green. Looking out onto the platform from her seat, Eve noticed several couples had got off the train. They were probably eloping to get married, she thought. Gretna Green was well known for conducting hasty marriages for underage English folk: in England the law required parental consent to marry before the age of twenty-one, but Scotland had no such restrictions. She watched these young people about her age, sparkling with excitement and anticipation. Then the conductor blew his whistle and the train lurched forward onto the last leg of the journey, whipping her stomach into a muddle of nerves and eagerness of a completely different kind.

She took a map from her bag and discovered that she was only fifty miles away from her destination. She'd been excited when the SOE told her she'd be training in Scotland; it was somewhere she'd never visited. She folded the map and concentrated on the unfamiliar view. The train picked up speed and the lush countryside flashed by her window. Dry stone walls bordered rolling green fields, where sheep dotted the landscape. In the distance she could see mountains climbing into thickening clouds, heavy with rain.

An elderly woman who had boarded the train at Gretna Green took the seat opposite Eve. She noisily rummaged around in her handbag and pulled out an apple.

"Would you like one, dear? I brought plenty with me."

"Thank you," Eve said, taking it.

"Where are you off to?"

"I'm visiting my uncle and aunt in Dumfries. Auntie isn't very well. I'm going to help out." She bit into the apple, thinking how easily the lie slipped off her tongue.

The woman reached up and removed her felt hat. She put it on her lap and folded her hands over it as if settling in for a good gossip. She leaned forward in her seat, unable to disguise her nosiness.

"Och, perhaps I know them. I'm from Dumfries myself," the woman said in a broad Scottish accent. She looked at Eve expectantly.

"I don't think so. They have a smallholding out on the moors. They don't get into town very often," she said, not wanting to engage her any further. She'd met her kind of woman before and knew that she'd wheedle every bit of information out of her, if she let her.

"Well, I hope that a wee slip of a lass like yourself will be able to survive out there. It's tough living. You'll be needing some warm clothes."

"I'm sure I'll be fine," Eve replied. She took out her map again, pretending to study it. The woman huffed and sat back in her seat.

It was late afternoon when the train slowly screeched into the station.

"Dumfries! Dumfries!" the guard shouted as he passed

through the train. "All change here for Glasgow. Dumfries!"

Eve quickly gathered her suitcase, hold-all, and handbag, hurrying off the train before her curious travel companion could follow her. Reaching in her pocket, she handed the inspector her ticket and made her way across the footbridge into the station building. Men and women in newly acquired uniforms milled around, saying goodbye to their families and loved ones. In the corner of the terminal, she saw *"Harrison"* scribbled on a piece of cardboard held high in the air.

Weaving her way through the crush of bodies, she found a soldier who was busy looking around him. "That's me," she said, pointing to the sign.

"I'm Bert," the soldier said, extending his hand. "I'm glad you found me, Miss. I've never seen so many people. It looks like everyone has signed up. Come on, then. Let me take your suitcase and we'll find my van. I'll be taking you to the camp. It's about an hour away."

"Would you mind awfully, but I'm dying for a cup of tea and I'd like to freshen up a bit, too."

"There's no rush. I could do with a cuppa myself," the soldier said as he guided her towards the station café.

The grinding noise of the van's gears woke her and a jolt threw her sideways. As soon as she'd climbed into the passenger seat of the van earlier, she'd fallen asleep. Now they were bumping along a rugged track densely lined with rhododendrons and pine trees. Bert brought the truck to a shuddering stop outside a large stone building.

"You slept well!" he said, opening her door. "Welcome to paradise. This is HQ, and over there are the sleeping quarters." He pointed to a group of Nissen huts set out in military-style.

"I hope I wasn't snoring," Eve said sleepily.

"It happens to the best of us," he replied, grinning.

She climbed out of the van in front of the whitewashed stone building, its long, paned windows overlooking the loch. A stream gurgled nearby, meandering its way until opening into the vast expanse of water. In the early evening light, she saw someone fishing from a rowboat in the distance. On the far bank, a hillside of purple heather lay like a soft blanket set out for a picnic, and rocky highlands towered behind heavy clouds, barely visible. Suddenly the wind picked up, creating ripples that crumpled the water's surface. A soft rain started to fall, and as it touched the ground, a musty smell of peat and earth rose into the air. Bert was right: this was paradise.

The next morning, she reported to the Operations Room in the main building. Drummond was dressed in a brown suit, not his Royal Air Force uniform. Eve raised her eyebrows.

"I can see that you're confused I'm wearing civvies. The SOE have officially assigned me to lead the operation of agents in the Rhône-Alpes region of France. I'm no longer in the RAF, but now belong to what's known as Churchill's Army. Please sit down." He pointed to the chair on the other side of his desk.

"As you know, we have recruited you for your glove-making skills, and because you are a bilingual French/English speaker. What you don't know is that Bertrand Dupuis, your uncle, gave us your name. He operates a Resistance network, using his glove-making factory as cover."

"My *tonton*—Bertrand Dupuis? My parents certainly never knew anything about this. They would have told me. Is he safe?"

"No one is safe. Your uncle is a very brave man. 'La Ganterie Dupuis' is the base for a network to help both the Resistance and the Allies. We are lucky to have him on board. He's assisted us greatly already."

"I suppose there can't be many bilingual glovemakers

around; that's why he suggested me," she said. "But I'm surprised he didn't discuss this with my family first."

"Yes, Eve, you're unique. But this operation is top secret, which is why few people know about it; your uncle understands that. We've also been lucky to find another special young lady who will be your partner. She's a mechanic and a French speaker. She'll be arriving tomorrow. You'll both be trained in radio operations, secret messaging techniques, survival, and weapons training. We have all the personnel in place to teach you exactly what you need to know. Your rare skills, and your partner's, will provide you with excellent cover to carry out your roles as secret agents. We believe no one is likely to suspect you, but your connection with your uncle will have to remain a secret."

Eve nodded her head. "What exactly will I be doing?"

Drummond stood and paced back and forth. "Let me first explain to you the situation in France," he said.

"The Germans now occupy much of France. The country is separated into two zones: the Occupied Zone and the Free Zone. The Vichy government is working under German rule. Until recently, Grenoble had been in the Free Zone. In the past month, the Italian army has taken control of the city, but now the German army is inching closer. The situation is reaching a crucial stage, accelerated by the Allied forces' new plans to defeat the enemy in France. The Prime Minister has determined that Resistance forces in France are central to the campaign, with the Allies financing them and supplying arms. He's putting much faith in their ability to defend the region and to sabotage German infiltration. We're making regular weapons drops into France, along with boots and clothing. Unfortunately, not all reach the intended destination, and much confusion is hampering the effort. Many weapons are damaged on arrival. That's where your partner's skill as a mechanic will be used. Her knowledge of British and American weapons will be invaluable to the Resistance fighters.

"You must understand that we're sending you into a complicated situation. The area to the southwest of Grenoble is a mainly mountainous one, until now remaining relatively untouched by German invasion. However, a law has been enacted in agreement with the Vichy government: *'Le Service du Travail Obligatoire'* means that all men born between 1920 and 1922 must register for work in Germany. There has been little resistance in this remote area to the German occupation of France. In fact, most local people are loyal to Marshal Petain and his Vichy government. But now, town workers and peasants in the countryside are rebelling against the new ruling. Small groups of young men who are refusing to comply are forming their own Resistance groups, hiding out in the mountains of the Vercors. According to intelligence reports, there's conflict between the different partisan groups due to poor discipline and management. Making things worse, military supplies are not reaching the correct parties on the ground. We need better organization if the plan to prevent further German occupation is to succeed, and the Allies have a plan in place. They are at this moment training specialist military personnel who will eventually infiltrate the area to train and oversee the growing numbers of guerilla fighters.

"Locals are suspicious of the *Maquis*, as these Resistance groups are known. They don't know who to trust, and there are reports that Vichy loyalist French spies have penetrated some cadres. We know that Communists are working alongside partisan groups, but they also have their own objectives."

Eve ran her hand through her hair and sighed. She already knew about *"Le Service du Travail Obligatoire"* from her mother, but that was about it. She hadn't considered the repercussions, or the different factions operating in France.

"As a courier your task is to form liaisons with the correct groups and create a strong line of communication. Your uncle will be able to guide you with regards to that. You will maintain radio contact with the SOE, passing on and receiving important messages.

"My dear, I have every belief that you are up to this important work. We will hone your language skills and you will receive excellent training in everything you need to know. If you don't pass the necessary requirements for the mission, though, we won't be able to send you to France."

Drummond's words buzzed in her ears. She was committed to her new role; failure was not a word that she would even consider.

"I'll do my best not to let you down, Sir."

The first few days of training included a survival course in the wilderness, during which Eve soon discovered that the blissful surroundings were anything but idyllic. She wasn't sure which was more difficult to endure, the course or the deceptive environment; lack of food left her dizzy and weak, and bites from angry swarms of midges turned her tender skin into a red dot-to-dot puzzle. The unrelenting rain on the day of the low rope course was almost her undoing.

"Look sharp, Harrison," the Sergeant barked. "If you're last back to camp, you know it'll be latrine duty or a swim across the loch."

When she emerged from under the roping, she took off her soaking wet boots and then her socks, trying to wring them out before setting off again. The sodden clothing was making it difficult to move. She stood in front of the Sergeant in a jumpsuit that clung to her like a soggy bath towel.

"Your little, tiny toes got wet, did they? I haven't got time for girlie girls. I'm not going to be with you to babysit where you're going. I don't know why they keep sending me a bunch of wee lasses just out of kindergarten. Get a move on, sweetheart, and stop faffing about!"

"Yes, Sarg. Sorry, Sarg."

She tried her best not to shiver as she put her socks and boots back on. Fueled by anger at the man's words, and mad at herself for almost failing the course, she eyed the first obstacle again. The sheer brick wall loomed ahead, as daunting as it had been the first time. She gritted her teeth, determined to force her body over the barrier.

Eve tossed and turned. It was impossible to sleep with rain battering the aluminum roof of the Nissen hut, and her muscles ached constantly. She secretly wished she was in her own bed, with her dad bringing her a hot cup of cocoa to help her doze off. Thinking about him made her heart ache, too. She thought she'd been so brave by telling him what she wanted to do; but now, after she'd persuaded him, she'd trained for something completely different. And she couldn't even tell him the truth.

Yet she knew she was doing the right thing. The opportunity to serve her country was too important to turn down, and she was proud of being chosen. Not only would she be doing her bit for England, but she would also be a vital part of the war effort in France, where her mother's family was suffering. She was a jumble of nerves and excitement as she imagined joining her uncle for their heroic cause.

Keeping it from her family in Worcester was excruciating, though. Their goodbyes had been rushed and she felt guilty for her deception. She could still see them in her mind: her mum, dad, and Frankie waving on the platform as her train departed. Now she imagined them playing cards together in the little flat above the shop, with no idea of what she was doing or where she was going.

"Are you awake, Sylv?"

Sylvie, lying huddled in the next bed, groaned and sat up.

"Yes. I can't sleep either with this racket. Whoever makes

tin roofs deserves the sack. How you haven't punched Sarg yet, I don't know. That man is such a bully, the way he talks to you. How do you always stay so calm and serene?"

"Serene—you're joking. Have you seen the state of me? I detest that man. He even calls me sweetheart. Bloody cheek. I certainly wouldn't want him kissing me goodnight." She hummed the first bars of the popular song "Kiss me goodnight, Sergeant Major" and giggled.

"You're funny! But I couldn't agree more. I'd rather French kiss an old donkey than him," Sylvie said.

"For a moment, I didn't think I was going to make the survival course—but I'll never let him get inside my head, even if he thinks he can break me."

"Well, now you know how to break him."

Eve laughed. "I must say the man has taught us well. My dad would be gobsmacked that I can now dislocate someone's kneecap with my foot, and I know exactly the best place to stab someone to death. I hope I never have to, though."

"I know what you mean. My brothers will never believe that I can strip down a sub-machine gun in five minutes. They'd love to be playing around with guns. When I was thirteen, my dad taught me how to take apart an engine in his garage. He'd taught all my brothers, so he didn't see why I shouldn't learn, too—six brothers I've got. It's nothing but rough-housing day and night where I live. I've learned to give as good as I get."

Eve's mission partner was a young woman called Sylvie Smith. Over the weeks, the two girls had become inseparable. They discovered that both their mothers were French, and this connection became an unspoken bond, separating them from the other recruits. Sylvie was tall, with long blonde hair always tied back in a ponytail. Although she was much stronger physically than Eve, as the endurance course had proved, they shared the same steely determination to succeed in everything they undertook. The sergeant in charge, despite his seeming irritation with Eve, had nicknamed them "The Plucky Hens." He was the most impressed by the girl's grit during simulated interrogations, when "*les Boches*" dragged them from their beds in the middle of the night. They'd both remained tight-lipped to protect each other.

"Do you have a boyfriend at home, Eve?"

"No, not really. I was walking out with someone, but he was called up. I felt I should write to him because he's away from home, but I've never heard back. Someone told me he was seeing other girls at the same time as me, so he's no great loss. I just hope he's safe though."

"I don't have one either. Just as well if we're going to be sent abroad. We should get some shut-eye." She yawned loudly.

"Are you scared, Sylv?" Eve asked.

"Yes, I am a bit. I can't wait to get out of this place though. We'll find out the details of our mission tomorrow."

"I can't believe France could possibly be any worse. I can't wait to sort those bloody German bastards out. I just hope I've passed the test," Eve whispered back with a bravado that she didn't quite feel.

"Eve Harrison. Those are strong words from such a pretty mouth."

The next morning, they reported to the Briefing room in the old hunting lodge. A secretary in uniform sat behind a typewriter, efficiently tapping away at the keys, while an older woman in faded floral overalls was busy handing out cups of tea from a trolley. Charts and maps covered the walls.

Drummond stood up as they entered the room. He lifted two chairs from a pile stacked on the wall and put them down. Then he placed his leather briefcase on the table and took out a sheaf of paperwork.

"I am happy to tell you that you have both successfully completed the final stage of your training. Over the past six weeks, you've learned new skills, including how to transmit messages in code and to silent kill. As you know, women in the Armed Forces are not permitted to go into frontline combat. However, our guidelines are looser. Your particular assignment is not to kill, but the occasion may arise when you need to defend yourselves or someone else."

He stood up and pointed to an area on a map of France.

"This is where your drop will be. There's a hidden airstrip near Saint-Julien-en-Vercors. Agents will take you from there to Villard-de-Lans, where you will stay with Monsieur Agard and his wife. He's a member of the Resistance." He indicated again on the chart with his stick. "And here is Grenoble, where you will travel to the following day. Monsieur Dupuis will be expecting you."

Sylvie put up her hand.

"Yes, dear?"

"How will we get to Grenoble from the town?"

"Monsieur Agard drives the bus that goes from Villard-de-Lans to Grenoble. Monsieur Dupuis will meet you at his factory in Grenoble. All the details are in your travel envelope, which you will need to study before you leave. You will also find your identity cards and sufficient cash for your mission. You will leave all your personal effects behind. Clothes have been sent from France for you. Everything will be in order—your cards with your new names will be marked that you have crossed the Demarcation line.

"To the outside world, you will be two friends from Paris looking for work, as a glovemaker and a mechanic. You have been given different surnames for obvious reasons, and although Monsieur Dupuis knows your identity, no one else will. You'll continue to speak to each other in French; any lapse into British language or habits would be extremely dangerous. You're now French women. It's crucial that you follow your training down to the tiny details."

He stood up while gathering his paperwork together to put it back in his briefcase. He clicked the clasps shut with a loud snap. The briefing was over.

"I have every confidence that your training will stand you in good stead for your mission. But this is very risky. I can't guarantee your safety."

"When will we leave for France, Sir?" Eve asked.

"You'll travel to London tomorrow and then on to RAF Newmarket, where a Lysander from the RAF Special Duties squadron will fly you to the French Alps. Weather conditions look good for the night flight. French agents will be on the ground in Saint-Julien-en-Vercors to pick you up. Good luck, ladies."

Eve managed to make a phone call home before leaving the training camp for the trip to Newmarket. She'd waited in line for half an hour before being able to use the only phone available to the recruits. She sat down in the small cubicle and pulled the curtain across, shielding her from curious ears and eyes. She tipped all the coins from her purse onto her lap and picked up the phone.

"What number please?" the switchboard operator asked.

"Worcester 1481," she replied. She inserted the pennies into the slot.

"Putting you through," the woman said, after a moment.

When she heard her mother's voice, she pressed button A and listened as the money slid into the receptacle below, connecting her.

"*Maman*, it's me," Eve said. She pictured her mother standing on the cracked linoleum in the little dark hallway, holding the handset away from her ear like she always did. The thought brought a lump to her throat.

"Where are you, *chérie*?" Véronique shouted into the phone. "We miss you. You've been gone for over six weeks."

"I'm sorry but I'm not allowed to tell you where I am. I'm doing okay. I'm still training, I don't know when I'll be home. How's Dad?"

"He's fine. Grumbling as usual about too much work—you know what he's like. How do you like being a nurse?"

"It's not quite what I expected," she replied, crossing her fingers behind her back.

"Well, I'm glad at least you're in England and they're not sending you off somewhere, like they did with your friend Ethel's dad. He was working on something top secret. He's gone missing."

"Missing? Where?"

"They don't now. They got a telegram last week—they're all in a terrible state."

"Have you seen Ethel?"

"She was in the Post Office the other day with her mum. They both looked in a bad way."

"That's awful—give her a hug from me when you see her next. Give Dad my love and tell Frankie I've written to him. I've sent him some new 'knock-knock' jokes I've heard—you know how he loves them."

"It's cheered me up no end just hearing your voice, *chérie*, but I wish I could see you."

"Sorry, *Maman*—I've got to go. I wish I could talk longer, but other people are waiting to use the phone and my money's about to run out. I love you. See you soon." The phone line crackled.

"Eve?"

"I love you, *Maman*. Bye..." Eve said, blinking hard to clear the tears that were misting her eyes.

There were three sharp pips. Then the line went dead.

CHAPTER 6

EVE AND GEORGINA
Worcester, 2016

Outside, the afternoon produced an unexpected sun shower; rain was falling, but the sky was bright. Eve and Georgina sat in the living room, where the shimmery light filtered through the cracks in the wood shutters, along with the rhythmic swish of car tires on the wet road and the muffled voices of passersby on the sidewalk. Dust motes flickered in the air, somehow intensifying Eve's story. She lay back in her favorite armchair with her feet resting on a stool, her oxygen bottle alongside her. Every now and then she put the mask to her face and inhaled deeply.

"You didn't even get to say a proper goodbye to your family before you left," Georgina said.

"It wasn't easy. My parents weren't happy either; they couldn't understand why I couldn't train to be a nurse locally. But it wasn't so unusual then to move to different parts of the country. Most girls I knew joined the WAAFs or the Wrens and left home too. Everyone wanted to do their bit. My best friend

Ethel was in the Land Army and worked on a fruit farm outside town."

"Is she still alive?"

"As a matter of fact, she is. She lives in a nursing home in Cheltenham. Her father died in a prisoner-of-war camp in Japan. Her mother never got over losing him, and Ethel looked after her until she died. She never married."

"Did you ever tell her what you did in France?"

"No. I couldn't burden her with that. We still chatted on the phone until last year, but they say she has Alzheimer's disease now. She's the last of my generation."

"I've been wondering if you ever became a nurse."

"No, I didn't. Those dreams never stood a chance. After I came back from France, I had Angela and all the bother with Tom; then my dad got sick. He died of lung cancer. The doctor said he probably got it from the dye we used in the glove-making process. He never wore a mask like he was supposed to. *Maman* was always on at him to wear one. But he smoked a pipe as well, so I'm sure that contributed. Anyway, after he passed away, *Maman* ran the factory and I worked in the shop. I kept the business going for many years and my hopes of nursing faded away."

"Did you ever regret that you never fulfilled your dreams?"

"Regret is not a useful emotion. It can be destructive—I learned that early on. I'll always feel immense sadness at the way things turned out, so knowing that I did the right thing being a secret agent is something which I'll always cling onto. My generation all sacrificed something, but we did it to help save all those poor people who lost everything; some people just gave up more than others."

"That's so tragic, especially as you've had no one to share your pain with all these years. You're amazing—so brave. Did you at least get some therapy from a counsellor when you came home?" Georgina asked.

"No, dear. We all just got on with our lives."

Eve had the same faraway look in her eyes that Georgina had noticed several times over the last couple of weeks.

"War is a bad thing, but we had to stand up to Hitler. We couldn't let him get away with what he was doing. I can't feel sorry for myself when so many people suffered terribly. There's always someone worse off than you. I was just grateful to be alive."

Georgina was in awe of Eve's stoicism and of the risks she took at such a young age. She thought how comfortable her own life had been so far. She understood now that this comfort was possible because of the sacrifices her grandmother's generation had made. It made her feel ashamed that she'd taken her lifestyle for granted.

She got up and looked out of the window for a moment. The rain had stopped, and a light mist rose off the cobblestones in the street. In her mind's eye, she could see her grandmother walking over those same stones, with Frankie and her parents, holding hands, making their way to the train station. The image brought a lump to her throat. Swallowing hard to stop herself from crying, she headed for the kitchen.

"Would you like a cup of tea? Eileen said that Kate from two doors down dropped off a chocolate cake for you this morning. How about a slice?"

"You know me and my sweet tooth. You're in for a treat, she's an excellent baker."

In the small galley, she put on the kettle to boil. She took two china teacups and saucers from the cupboard over the sink and placed them on a tray. The chocolate cake looked splendid, with swirls of frosting and a Cadbury's Flake sprinkled over the top. Cutting a large slice for her grandmother, she took a smaller one for herself. Since arriving in Worcester, she was eating far more sweet things than she had ever done in New York. She'd forgotten how the Brits loved their afternoon tea with cake or cookies, and now she too was hooked on the ritual. Once the tea was brewed, she took the tray into the living room and placed it on the coffee table. She placed the teacup and saucer on a side table next to Eve, along with a piece of cake on a plate.

"I've never been to Scotland. It sounds breathtaking," Georgina said, as she tucked into her slice of the cake. "I'd love to see where you did your training."

"You'd like the countryside in Scotland. Perhaps you'll visit one day. I often thought of going back to see if the old lodge was still there, but I read that it has become an outward-bound school for juvenile delinquents. I wonder if they have as tough a time there as I did."

Georgina put down her empty plate and licked her fingers. "That was delicious. I've been meaning to ask you if there's somewhere I can run around here—like a track. She patted her stomach.

"Are you worried about putting on weight? If you must run, there are quite a few trails around and about town. There's a pretty walk along the canal. I'm sure that's where all the young things run or jog these days. Do you remember, I took you there to feed the ducks?"

"Was it that time when we came over to look at boarding schools? Mum went off to London and left me with you. I must have been eight or nine."

"Yes, you were such a precious little thing with an American accent. I couldn't understand a word you said!" Eve took another bite of cake. "Now, tell me, has that boyfriend of yours phoned you yet?" she asked as she wiped her mouth with a paper napkin.

Georgina sighed. "No, he's definitely dumped me. I thought I'd miss him more than I do, though. It's funny how life turns out, isn't it? If I hadn't come here to visit you, then we'd probably still be together. Just trundling along."

She reached for Eve's cup and poured more tea from the pot. She automatically sugared it to Eve's liking, before placing it back on the table.

"When you fell in love, did you know right away?"

"Oh, my dear. I knew from the minute I saw him. That doesn't mean to say that the feeling doesn't grow over time, though. Some of the best marriages are based on strong friendships."

"I know I've never been in love. I can't have been because no breakup has upset me that much. I mean, I'm not that upset about Marco—just a bit miffed how it ended. I hate bad feelings."

"Well, I can guarantee some young man is going to fall head over heels for you one day, so don't fret." The old lady smiled affectionately at her granddaughter.

"You know, Grandy, I've never talked to my mother like I'm talking to you. You've so much wisdom to share. I wish I'd spent more time with you over the years."

"I do too, dear. I never had conversations like this with your mother either. I'm glad you're here."

The bone china cups, saucers, and plates clinked tunefully as Georgina cleared away the tea things.

"I'll just go and wash these up. When I come back, I want to hear about how you met the love of your life."

"I'll get to that, all in good time. I've never told anyone about him before, but I know you're the right person to share this with. It's painful to remember."

CHAPTER 7

EVE AND SYLVIE
France, 1943

After a long train journey and a rickety ride in an Airforce bus to Newmarket, the girls found themselves in the care of a handsome young pilot who introduced himself as Bob.

"Meet 'Lizzie,' the Lysander that will take us to France," he said, as he tenderly stroked the wing of the plane. "She only flies on a moonlit night. It's quite a romantic ride. I do this all the time, so you're in safe hands."

He pulled on his flight cap and gloves before helping the girls into the aircraft.

"Don't forget to buckle up after you sit down—it does get a bit bumpy."

The pilot navigated his way helped by the brightness of the moon, using only topographical features, a map, and a compass to guide him to France. He followed wide rivers twinkling in the moonlight, with tributaries spread out in front of him like arteries in a body. Facing backwards on a narrow wooden bench, the girls viewed the landscape sliding away from them, leaving their homes and all that was familiar behind. Ahead, the snowcapped peaks of the Alps awaited, their icy crowns encircled by a sprinkling of stars. In the confined space of the Lysander's rear cockpit, they sat next to each other and silently waited.

The nearly four-hour flight frightened Eve more than she had expected; she didn't find it romantic at all. The deafening drone of the engine hurt her ears. She clenched her jaw tight in fear, all the while swallowing to overcome the bile rising in her throat, caused by the constant buffeting of the airplane's wings and the stuffy, smelly, and hot atmosphere. Anxiety and dizziness mingled together, and the sausage sandwich that she'd eaten in the NAAFI earlier that evening churned uncomfortably in her stomach.

Inside the protective padded suit provided by the RAF, her body was screaming to be let out. Sylvie, too, despite her tough exterior, sat slumped on the tiny bench. To pass the time and take their minds off their discomfort, they started to sing.

Finally, the young pilot's voice shouted above the throbbing of the plane's engine.

"Ladies, we're almost there. Remember your training. When we land, open the hatch, and roll out as quickly as you can. Don't forget to throw your bags out first. There won't be much time before I have to take off again."

As the plane got closer to the ground, Sylvie prised Eve's fingers off her right hand and whispered, "I'll be right behind you."

There was no sound except for the whirring of the plane's propeller and the low putter of the engine as it landed on the short ribbon of land. Agents on the ground had lit flares moments earlier, directing Bob to the meadow. Tall pine trees lined the makeshift runway, making it a difficult maneuver, but the skillful pilot had found his way to this and other runway strips many times before, dropping supplies and picking up pilots shot down over enemy territory. He liked to joke that it was just like driving the Number 23 bus down Clapham High Street.

Sylvie opened the hatch and threw her suitcase onto the ground, then grabbed hold of Eve's suitcase and threw it out too. Eve hesitated for a moment before Sylvie gave her a shove with her foot, pushing her onto the grass below. She quickly followed, turning to close the hatch securely. As they lay still on the grass, they watched the plane disappear into the night sky above their heads, floating into the air towards the huge moon, like a moth fluttering towards a light bulb, leaving them behind to an uncertain fate.

Eve sat up and from the other side of the airstrip heard a muffled voice grunt, "*Dépêchez-vous!* Come with me—don't say a word."

A rush of adrenaline flowed through her stiff body, dissolving the fear that had coursed through her veins on the plane. She picked up her suitcase and, dropping low, ran across to the sound of the voice, Sylvie following close behind. Another man appeared from the shadows, quickly put out all the flares lining the airstrip, and followed the women back to a waiting farm truck. Neither Eve nor Sylvie had uttered a word.

"Welcome to France. We were expecting some *Rosbifs,* not British *adolescentes,*" the man joked. He chewed nervously on his rough-cut moustache before reluctantly removing his blue beret, revealing a bald head that seemed to shine in the moonlight. "My name is Albert, and this is *mon ami* Georges." He nodded over to a much younger man who had just lit a cigarette as he got into the driver's seat of a small Citroen *camionette.* The smokey aroma of the *Gauloises* cigarette hung in the night air, confirming that they were indeed on foreign soil.

"Georges will drive you to your destination where you'll spend the night. I'll be coming with you as far as Collard. I hope my wife has kept the bed warm for me." He winked at the girls, flinging their suitcases carelessly into the bed of the truck. He made a gallant gesture with his grimy hand, indicating that they would be sitting with their baggage. Eve used his shoulder to push herself into the truck. She settled herself down on a wooden box next to Sylvie.

The truck's engine coughed as it started up, and they set off up a rough narrow track guided only by the moon and starlit sky. Georges kept the headlights switched off, not wanting anyone to notice them. The van labored in first gear as it climbed up the steep road. He shifted into second, passing around tight hairpin bends with sharp drops to a gorge far below, before plunging into a hair-raising descent. The moonlight glimmered through the branches of spruce and beech trees, casting eerie shadows across the track, like the long fingers of a witch beckoning to them. A fox darted in front of the truck; the silver streaks of its tail illuminated in the brightness of the night. Snowcapped mountains towering above formed a silvery-white halo in the sky.

As the truck bumped its way down the twisting track, Georges whistled softly to himself. It was a tune that Eve's mother played on their piano; comforted by its familiarity, she hummed along with him. She tried to make out the landscape on the other side of the trees. The spicy smell of the spruce trees reminded her of their living room at Christmas time. She hugged herself, feeling a connection to home.

They'd traveled for a mile when Georges pulled up outside a stone-built shepherd's hut, with a sharply sloping roof and wood shuttered windows. The house sat invitingly on the roadside, with smoke curling from the chimney and neatly stacked wood along one wall. Albert opened the passenger door.

"I'm getting out here," Albert whispered. "Good luck, ladies, and God bless you for coming to help us."

He closed the door of the truck and took a couple of paces to the front door of the hut. As he unlatched it, the door sprang open, and a brief ray of light splashed out onto the track; then all went dark in the road.

"Blimey—this is nothing like I imagined. The men here are a bit rough and ready, aren't they?" Eve whispered.

"Shush—we're meant to be speaking in French, remember." Sylvie let out a nervous giggle. "I can see what you mean though. Imagine having to get into bed with Albert. His poor wife." She wrinkled her nose.

"I always thought French men were meant to be wildly romantic, you know—like Maurice Chevalier," Eve said wistfully.

"And there was you thinking you were going to find us some handsome frogs in France," Sylvie teased.

"I did nothing of the sort." Eve nudged her friend in the ribs playfully.

They continued for another two miles. Georges navigated the switchbacks, shifting gear skillfully as they wound their way down the deeply wooded mountainside to the outskirts of a village. A signpost that read *"VILLARD-DE-LANS"* loomed out at them in the darkness. The narrow road curled through some more hairpin bends, passing by unlit houses, before opening into the center of the village square. Georges cut the engine, letting the truck silently coast by itself to a spot outside a building adorned with the sign: *"AUTOCARS – RENÉ AGARD ET FILS."*

"This is as far as I take you," he said. "Monsieur Agard is expecting you." He grabbed the cases out of the back of the truck.

"Merci, Georges." The girls picked up their suitcases. They'd taken off the cumbersome padded suits, revealing their French clothes supplied by the SOE. Eve's fondness for style left her disappointed with the dull brown coat nipped in at the waist that the SOE had chosen for her. Underneath she wore a brown skirt, a cream cotton blouse, and a brown knitted sweater. Sylvie's outfit was a gray coat, a blue skirt, and a navy

knitted short-sleeved top with a matching cardigan. Her long blonde hair was now cut into a bob, curling behind her ears to stop it from falling into her face. They both had on thick woolen stockings and sensible lace-up shoes.

A lone cat prowled across the dark square, making its way down a narrow alleyway next to the building. Every window was tightly shuttered to keep out the night air and intruders. Georges tapped quietly on the front door. The hinges creaked loudly, as a man wearing a shabby black suit and an oversized beret edged it open. His trousers hung loosely on his skeletal body, held up only by a thick piece of string. Recognizing Georges, he ushered them inside. *"Bonjour, Mesdemoiselles. Entrez."* He gave Georges a quick look and raised one eyebrow. Georges turned to look at him and shrugged his shoulders. He tipped his beret. *"Au revoir et bon courage.* I hope you know what you're doing."

A dim light bulb hanging from the ceiling revealed a long, narrow hallway paved with a slab stone floor worn smooth with age. Several pairs of heavy boots were lined up along one wall, with coats, scarves, and hats hanging from wooden pegs. The door to the right of the hallway was open and the girls followed Monsieur Agard into a small parlor. The Virgin Mary stared down at them from a picture above a wide, open fireplace where a log fire burned.

Although the girls had completed their immersion training and were both fluent in French, they didn't expect to feel quite so out of place. Monsieur Agard scratched his unshaven chin, then slowly shook his head with a look of disbelief in his eyes. *"Mon Dieu—*they're sending children to help us now. And we wanted men, not girls. We need experts who can help mend our broken weapons—not teenagers to make disgusting English tea!"

He swept his hands across his chest, making an exaggerated sign of the cross. Eve bristled at his remarks and his obvious disdain for them.

"I can assure you, Monsieur, that we can do everything that men can. Sylvie can fix anything, and we both know how to transmit messages, use explosives, and handle weapons. We're prepared to do everything it takes to free France from *les Boches*."

"Hmph!" he spluttered. "Well, whatever you know or don't know, you've got your work cut out for you. Most people don't even want to be freed, and half the time we don't even know who our enemy is. This is not a job for the faint-hearted and certainly not one for women—I don't know what they are thinking sending you."

The smell of garlic had settled into the fabric of the room, mixing with a bitter smell of something Eve didn't recognize.

"My wife has made some coffee for you, but if you would rather go straight to bed then I'll show you to your room."

"Just a glass of water, please," Eve said, really longing for a cup of tea.

"If that's all you want, I'll take your suitcases upstairs and my wife will get you some water. The less you know about us, the better for all of us. My bus will leave for Grenoble tomorrow afternoon, so get some rest now. The Italian garrison is on the outskirts of the village, but a few of the soldiers are billeted in some of my neighbors' houses. Luckily, they haven't bothered us so far. However, they will check your papers on the bus before we leave the village—please make sure that you have them ready. I hope you know what you have let yourselves in for."

CHAPTER 8

GEORGINA AND EVE
Worcester, 2016

"Were French men really that awful, Grandy? The way you described Albert wasn't very flattering and Monsieur Agard sounded horrid."

"No, dear. There were some extremely attractive men in France. I think I was expecting them all to be. Sylvie wasn't really interested in men though."

Georgina raised her eyebrows. "Do you mean she was gay?"

Eve whimpered slightly and turned her head away from Eve. "She was the loveliest and toughest woman I ever knew," she said, avoiding the question. "She always had my back. We were such good friends."

"What happened to her—is she still alive?"

Eve's eyes glistened as she continued to stare vacantly at the window. "No. She died." She fumbled with the drawer of her bedside table and took out a small envelope. Inside was a black and white photo that she handed to Georgina, along with a brown, shriveled sprig of a shrub. "That was taken just before we left for France. She'd just given me this piece of white heather for good luck."

Georgina stared at the crinkled photo of the two girls leaning against a drystone wall with their arms around each other. "I can't believe you went off to France in the war. Does Mum know any of this?"

"No, I've never told anyone until now. But the future is where your mother's heart has always taken her. I doubt if she would be interested in my past. It was risky, but when you're young, you think you're invincible—nothing can hurt you. We were swept up by duty and service to our country; everyone was then."

Georgina looked again at the photo that her grandmother still had in her hand. "Can you tell me what happened to Sylvie? Does the note I found have something to do with her?"

"I'll tell you about the note when I'm ready," Eve said.

"What's that you're looking at, Grandy?"

Eve was holding a scrap of paper in her hand. "It's Luc. It's a sketch of him. I'm not an artist but working on it helped me picture him in my mind. It's the only image I have of him. I've tried to draw him again over the years, but I can't get it right." Eve struggled to breathe, and her face turned pale. "I feel quite dizzy. I don't want to talk anymore, dear. I think I need a nap."

Georgina stood up and poured her grandmother a glass of water from the jug on the bedside table. "Yes, get some rest. Perhaps some warm milk will help you sleep; I'll fetch some," she said.

She felt her phone vibrate. Seeing that it was Camilla calling her, she let it go to voicemail.

Later, after her grandmother had finally drifted off to sleep, she closed the bedroom door quietly behind her and sat down on the top step of the stairs to call Camilla back.

"Well, it's been quite a week of revelations. It seems that Grandy was a courier for the Resistance in France during World War Two. I'd been looking for an old box that she wanted, and the story came pouring out. She found a note that she'd never seen before. It's really upset her a lot. I'll tell you all about it when I see you."

"That's amazing! Has your mum shown up yet?"

"No, but she called me today. She's not coming back for a while. She didn't even wait to hear about Grandy. She'd rather stay in Greece and look after some man she's just met."

"That sounds just like her. I called to see if you'd like to come for the afternoon tomorrow to meet the children—stay for dinner. I know Matt would like to see you too."

"I'd love to. I'll check if it's okay with Eileen. I'm worried about Grandy. She's overdone things today."

"I understand. Just let me know when you can."

Going back into her grandmother's room, Georgina went over to sit on the edge of the bed. Eve had fallen asleep clutching the photo and her drawing of Luc. She carefully took the mementos out of her hand and placed them on the nightstand.

Turning off the main road, the Uber drove into a smaller one that led to the village of Callow Bottom. Georgina leaned forward in her seat and pointed to the first house in the lane.

"That's it, I think," she said to the driver.

On the other side of a tall, ivy-covered brick wall, tightly trimmed boxwood balls lined a gravel driveway, leading to the handsome Georgian manor where Camilla and Matt lived. Camilla had told her that Matt, a property developer, had renovated the house, while his team of landscape gardeners had planted the gardens. Georgina sank back into her seat as they pulled into the entrance. The car swept past manicured lawns and herbaceous borders already in full bloom, before coming to a stop in a small courtyard, where two stone lions guarded the front door.

Georgina looked around admiringly. "Cam has done very well for herself," she thought. Camilla's posh country home and successful life as a senior financial analyst with an investment banking firm could not have been more different from Georgina's hotel-dwelling, jet-setting career-woman's lifestyle in New York. From Moreton College she'd attended Nottingham University, earning a first-class degree in economics. She'd worked her way up the executive ladder with two small children to cope with, making Georgina now realize that her own life had been more or less handed to her on a platter.

A delicious aroma wafted from the shiny blue Aga in Camilla's open-plan kitchen. The room was oversized, divided by a large, granite-topped island, with two armchairs and a sofa next to a fireplace in another section. At the far side of the room was a large slab dining table, made from the wood of a local oak tree that Matt had cut down while working on one of his development properties. Building blocks, puzzles, toy cars, and the general detritus of life with small children lay strewn all over the honey-colored wood flooring.

"I thought you'd invited me for dinner, not a play date!" Georgina called over to Camilla, while untangling her baby Daisy's sticky fingers from her hair. The plump toddler, clinging to Georgina like an octopus, grinned back, jam from her teatime sandwich still smeared on her face. The brightly colored castle that Georgina had spent most of the afternoon building sat triumphantly on the floor in front of them. She leaned back on her heels admiring her handiwork, when

Henry decided to throw a ball at it, reducing the work of art to small pieces.

"What did you do that for?" she asked, dismayed. She watched as he continued to demolish her carefully constructed French chateau, kicking the bricks around the room.

"Color with me, now!" the little boy squealed. He grabbed her hand, dragging her over to the table littered with coloring books and crayons.

"Enough," she said. "I need a break." She fell, spread-eagled, into one of the comfy armchairs, with the tiny girl still wrapped around her, the silk blouse she was wearing crumpled and now splodged with Daisy's jammy fingermarks.

"They're always fractious at this time of day," Camilla shouted out as she added butter to a pan of mashed potatoes. "Florence is going to give them a bath soon. She's loved having a bit of a break today. I just heard Matt drive in. We'll have dinner soon. I've made a cottage pie."

"I played with Ben a bit when he was younger," Georgina said. "None of my other friends have kids, so I don't get much practice at this. It's exhausting. I have absolutely no idea how you do it."

"I know, I'm extremely lucky to have help. My job can be demanding at times, but Matt and I are a team. I never thought you'd be so good with kids, though."

"Thanks a lot!"

Florence bathed the children before going up to her room with a tray of food to watch TV, leaving Matt to deal with his son. Henry was still overexcited and didn't want to go to bed.

"Quiet time, I think," Matt said. "What story do you want tonight?"

"I want Georgie to read me a story! The one about the caterpillar."

"Not tonight, old chap. You've worn her out."

"That's alright Matt, I'd love to read to him. Run and fetch the book, Henry," Georgina said, smiling.

Henry came back with the storybook he'd chosen and snuggled next to Georgina in the oversized armchair.

"Give me a kiss goodnight," she said, when she finished the story. "I think it's time for bed now."

The little boy put his arms around her neck and pecked her on the cheek. Matt scooped up his son and tossed him over his shoulder. As he marched out of the room, Georgina could hear the pair singing loudly.

"What a great guy, Cam. He's always been a hunk and now he's a great dad, too."

Camilla grinned. "I know. I'm lucky, aren't I?"

"I hope I have a life like this one day," Georgina thought to herself wistfully.

A few minutes later, Matt came downstairs, having finally succeeded in getting Henry to sleep.

"Well, you were a great hit, Georgie. Henry can't stop talking about you."

Camilla thrust a can of beer into his hand.

"Thanks, love," he said, taking a long, satisfying mouthful. "Georgie, I hear your grandmother has been telling lots about her life in World War Two."

"Yes, she's finally decided to talk about it after all these years. She'd always felt she couldn't before because she'd signed The Official Secrets Act, but it's such a long time ago now." She picked up her wine glass. "I never even knew she made gloves—like, she made them from scratch! I always thought that she just sold gloves from a dingy old shop. And I never knew Worcester was a center for glove-making in England back in the day."

Camilla rolled her eyes. "Where were you in history lessons at school? I thought everyone knew that. Mrs. Baxter used to go on and on about it. Her family was in the glove-making business too."

"Oh, I don't remember anything about History class. I do remember her though. Wasn't she that fat old thing with a moustache and bad breath? I don't think she liked me very much."

"That's because you were always messing about. I remember she caught you passing around a rude picture you drew of her."

"You're right, I was pretty bad—it was fun though, wasn't it?"

"It's a wonder you weren't expelled, the things you got up to. Remember when you snuck out to meet those boys in the pub and didn't come back until the following morning?"

"You wouldn't come with me. That seems like a lifetime ago. So, Clever Clogs, tell me what you learned about glove-making in Worcester."

"Let's see, I think during the eighteenth and nineteenth centuries almost half of all glovemakers in England worked in and around Worcester."

"Yes, you're right, Cam," Matt said, leaning forward importantly. "But have you both heard of Dent's gloves? If I remember correctly, John Dent started his first glove making business in Wood Street in 1777. Another interesting little historical snippet is that Shakespeare's father was a tanner and glovemaker, just twenty miles from here."

Georgina rolled her eyes at Camilla. "All I thought Worcester was famous for was the sauce."

They chatted companionably as they ate their meal, and when they finished, went to sit down next to the fireplace. Camilla sipped her wine while she listened to Georgina talk some more about her grandmother. It occurred to her that this re-connection with the old lady, however late in the day, was exactly what Georgina needed to get her life on track and to grow roots. Over the years, she had felt sorry that her friend never had much of a relationship with her parents.

"Did you ever know your grandfather?" Matt shouted. He was in the kitchen rinsing dirty plates under the tap, before loading them into the dishwasher. "Is it possible he's still alive?"

"I really don't know. I've never even been curious about my grandfather until now. Grandy says I look just like him."

"Matt, we should get Paul and Georgina together."

Matt sat down next to his wife and put his arm around her.

"Great idea!" He looked over at Georgina. "Paul works for one of those genealogy websites now. Remember, I went to Uni with him. When I spoke to him the other day, he sounded a bit down. He's just broken up with his girlfriend. He's coming to stay next weekend. Perhaps you'd like to come for dinner on Saturday night. You can tell him all about your grandmother, I'm sure he'll be fascinated. And you never know; you two might hit it off."

Camilla punched his shoulder. "It's a great idea about Paul doing some research but—you and your matchmaking, Matt! I'm sure the last thing Paul wants to do right now is get involved with someone else."

"You don't know that. Maybe he needs a bit of distraction." He winked at Georgina, before changing the subject.

"I can't believe your grandmother was an SOE operative. I was reading a story in the paper the other day about a spy in France," he said. "Apparently she was a genius at disguise and infuriated the Nazis. They couldn't catch her. Her story only came out a few years ago, after she had died, when her family found a suitcase full of paperwork revealing what she'd done. No one knew a thing about it. They thought she was a hairdresser."

"That sounds just like my Grandy," Georgina said proudly.

CHAPTER 9

EVE AND SYLVIE
France, 1943

The girls finally fell into dreamless sleep as a rooster crowed outside their bedroom window, heralding a new day. The heavy shutters acted as a blackout. They had no idea of the time when Madame Agard finally woke them.

She carried a large enamel bowl and a pitcher of hot water which she put down on the chest of drawers with a thud. Her arms, sticking out of the sleeves of her drab cotton dress, looked like brittle twigs that could snap under the weight of the heavy jug.

"*Bonjour, bonjour,*" she said. The floorboards creaked noisily as she crossed the room to open their bedroom window. A stream of light flooded in, together with the rhythmic cooing of a pigeon which echoed around the room. "I'm sorry to wake you, but if you're to travel to Grenoble today, you need to get yourselves ready. It's already after eleven."

Eve was completely disoriented. She couldn't remember where she was until she saw Sylvie lying next to her. The events of the previous day came flooding back to her. She threw off the feather eiderdown, swung her legs over the side of the bed, and stood up. With the shutters now wide open, she went over to the window to look out. There was a walled backyard, surrounded by houses on each side, which had been put to good use. Vegetables grew in neat rows, and chickens pecked lazily under the poles of beans and between rows of cabbages. The scene outside the window, framed by the rugged, snow-capped mountains that towered over the town, looked as if it belonged on a picture postcard. Eve couldn't help but think how different it was from home, and that her father would love to garden in such a setting.

"Get yourselves dressed and come downstairs. I have breakfast ready for you," Madame Agard said.

The bedcovers moved and Sylvie, who had been fast asleep, groaned. She breathed in the same pungent smell that had filled the house the previous night. "What's that smell and what time is it? Aaagh—I need more sleep." She turned over and pulled her pillow over her head.

"It is almost midday—up you get, lazybones. It's time we got moving. It's a gorgeous day outside," Eve said.

The air from the open window felt warm on her skin. After washing, she rubbed herself dry with a linen towel and got dressed. A pocket mirror hung on the wall next to the washstand. Squinting, she inspected her face. Her lips were dry; reaching for a tin of petroleum jelly, she dabbed them with the thick gel. Then she brushed her hair, smoothing it carefully before pushing it back with a tortoiseshell hairband. Sylvie sat watching her.

"Whose party are we going to?"

"What do you mean?" asked Eve.

"What are you dolling yourself up for?"

"I'm not. I'm just doing what I always do, silly."

"I never saw you tarting yourself up when we were training."

"Well, I was hardly likely to be doing that there, was I? I was covered in mud most of the time. Anyway, I want to look nice for my uncle," Eve said as she powdered her nose. She took out a lipstick that they'd both been given and twisted the top. It clicked open, revealing the cyanide pill that they'd been instructed to take should they be arrested. "I hope we never have to use this," she said.

"You're gloomy this morning. We've only just arrived, and you've already got us captured."

Sylvie got out of bed and quickly washed. She grabbed a pair of pants and the blouse she'd worn the day before. Picking up Eve's comb, she slicked her blonde hair off her face with a flourish. "That's me done. I'm used to my short hair now," she said. "How do I look? Good enough for your party?"

"You are an idiot!" Eve giggled.

Downstairs breakfast was waiting for them. Madame Agard had been out earlier to the *boulangerie* where she managed to buy two *baguettes* with the forged ration cards Eve had given her the night before. Madame Agard told the nosy baker's wife that her niece and a friend were visiting on their way to Grenoble, hoping to satisfy the old woman's curiosity. From there she had gone to a neighbor's house, where she traded tomatoes and beans for some creamy yellow butter. Now, she pressed the much-sought-after commodity into an earthenware crock and placed it beside a small pot of wild blueberry preserves on the breakfast table.

"This looks amazing, and how did you manage to get coffee?" Eve asked looking at the spread of food on the table. "We can't get it very easily in England."

"This isn't real coffee," the woman explained, as she poured the hot brown liquid and then steaming milk into two large bowls. "It's made from acorns. If we're lucky we can get chickpea coffee. I'm told chicory tastes much better though."

Eve spread her slice of *baguette* sparingly with the butter and blueberry preserves, realizing how precious this food was.

She took the *tartine* and dipped it into her bowl. The preserves and butter mingled with the ersatz coffee, creating a greasy, sweet mixture. She cradled the bowl in two hands and slurped hungrily. The warmth of the bowl was comforting. Sylvie, noticing that there wasn't a handle on the bowl, followed Eve's lead, first sipping the coffee, and then dunking the bread into the cup.

"This is delicious. I didn't think I was going to like acorn coffee," she said. "Thanks for sharing your food with us."

Eve ran her hand over the old, scratched pine table, wondering how many people had eaten there before.

"I've made some sandwiches for you," Madame Agard said. She produced two chunks of *baguette* spread with the precious butter and filled with a single slice of ham and little *cornichons*. She wrapped them in a white cloth and placed them in a basket together with a bottle of water. "The bus is leaving at one o'clock and my husband will be driving, as he does every day. The journey should take about two hours, as long as there are no new checkpoints along the road. We've heard that *les Allemandes* are slowly moving into the area, making travel more difficult."

The woman took out a handkerchief from her pocket and Eve watched as she fidgeted with it nervously.

"My husband is right. What you are doing is far too dangerous for young girls. May God be with you."

The bus was packed with passengers, but they managed to find two seats together across from an old lady carrying a basket of potatoes which she cradled on her lap like a baby. They put their suitcases in the rack above their heads. Two Italian soldiers had already boarded the bus and were passing from row to row, asking for everyone's identity papers. By the time they reached where Eve and Sylvie were sitting, Eve had her new card ready. She handed it to the younger of the two soldiers.

"Why are you traveling to Grenoble?" he asked.

"I'm looking for work in a glove factory," she said. Her lips felt as if they were glued together. She wasn't sure if she could get any more words out.

"What are you going to do there? I see you're from Paris."

"I'm a glovemaker. My friend Sylvie is a mechanic and can fix machinery." She took her lipstick out of her bag, smoothing it over her lips. The soldier kept staring at her. Sylvie pulled her card out of her bag and thrust it at him.

"I've never heard of a woman being a mechanic." He barely looked at Sylvie's papers; his eyes were fixed on Eve.

Eve tilted her head to one side. She gave him one of her smiles that usually had people smiling back. His mouth twitched. He handed the cards back to Sylvie.

"Well, everything looks in order, ladies. If you ever find yourself this way again, don't forget to look me up. I'd like a pair of those gloves." He gave Eve a sly wink before he turned to join his senior officer.

Eve dug Sylvie in the ribs with her elbow and whispered in French. "Don't you love my new lipstick?" She smacked her lips. "'*Rouge du soir*'—*C'est très chic. Maman* always says that with a nice smile you can win anyone over. With lipstick, it's even easier!"

Monsieur Agard maneuvered the bus down the steep, narrow road as ominous dark clouds scudded across the sky. Before long, heavy rain started to fall, making the route very slippery. The windshield wiper blades squeaked and groaned as they worked to keep the glass clear, but inside the windshield still steamed up. Eve gasped as René rubbed his sleeve against the glass. As he took his hand off the steering wheel, the bus wobbled alarmingly close to the side of the road and to the sheer drop below. A line of Mercedes approached from the opposite direction, bearing flags emblazoned with swastikas, each flapping heavily in the rain. René jerked on the handbrake to steady the bus as the first car sped past them imperiously honking its horn.

"*Mon Dieu*," he said. "They've arrived sooner than we thought."

The girls looked at each other in dismay. The intelligence given to them in Scotland had not indicated that German occupation of the region would be quite so imminent. Their mission, while just the same, had now become more danger-ous.

The rain had stopped by the time the bus pulled into Place La Grenette. René, alarmed at so much military activity, quickly directed the girls to Pont Saint-Laurent, eager to get back on his bus to start his return journey home.

"Cross over the bridge, turn left onto Quai Lambert. *La Ganterie Dupuis* is a brick building overlooking the river. You'll be stopped, and because you are carrying suitcases, they may give you a tough time. But if you act like you did on the bus, you'll be fine. Good luck," he said, turning quickly on his heels.

They walked slowly, weighed down by their suitcases. At the nearest checkpoint, a German soldier stood with his hand resting on the barrier and a rifle slung across his chest.

"Halt," he said, putting his hand in the air.

He had white-blonde hair just visible under his helmet and a smattering of wispy blonde stubble feathered his chin. Eve immediately raised her voice, pretending to have an argument with her friend.

"I told you not to pack so much—no wonder your arms are hurting. No! I won't swap suitcases with you. You're bigger than me!" She shoved her suitcase towards Sylvie. "Honestly, if I'd known you were going to be such a horrible travel companion, I'd never have agreed to come with you."

"What's all this noise about, young ladies? Where are you going?" the soldier asked. He smirked, enjoying their squabble.

"We're trying to find *La Ganterie Dupuis*. I'm a glovemaker and I'm looking for work," Eve said.

Sylvie ran the tip of her tongue over her lips. He watched her, mesmerized.

"Well, as much as I would like to watch a catfight, I have work to do. Move along now." He shouted out something in German to his colleague. They both laughed, leering at the girls as they walked through the barrier.

"Nice move, Sylv! You catch on quick."

Eve linked her arm through Sylvie's. She took a quick look over her shoulder. The soldiers were already busy questioning someone else.

They crossed over Le Pont Saint-Laurent. Farther down the river, a cable car swung in the air as it climbed up to what looked like an old fort set atop a promontory. Another car was making its descent towards the other side of the river. The sun was slowly sliding down behind the mountains, but there was still some warmth in the air, and the puddles on the cobblestones were starting to dry up.

The River Isère was on their right as they made their way up Quai Lambert. Faded awnings covered tables and chairs set out on the street, where men and women sat reading newspapers and drinking wine, defiantly ignoring the new German presence. It took about fifteen minutes to reach their destination. The sizable brick building that housed "*DUPUIS – Fabricant des Gants – Depuis 1820*" was topped with a handsome mansard roof, its long casement windows overlooking the river.

"This is it. I hope my uncle will be here to meet us."

Eve pushed open the heavy front door and stepped inside. To the right of a dark, wood-paneled hallway with a floor surfaced in polished red tiles, there was a door marked "*Bureau*" in gilt lettering. Sylvie put down her suitcase before knocking loudly. She opened the door. Nerves got the better of Eve, though, and she put her hand on her belly, as if that would stop its fluttering.

A buxom lady of about fifty sat behind a desk, with wire-framed glasses balanced on the tip of her nose and a knitted navy-blue cardigan draped over her shoulders, her pudgy fingers typing furiously. They stopped.

"*Bonjour.* Can I help you?" Her eyes were piercing like a crow's and darted over the girls from behind her glasses as she gave them the once-over.

"We're looking for Monsieur Dupuis."

"You must be the young ladies Monsieur Dupuis told me to expect. He's on the factory floor," she said. "I'll go fetch him. Take a seat over there." She pointed to a row of chairs leaned up against the wall. Taking her time, she heaved herself off the chair, waddling her way out of the room.

"I can't believe I'm really here," Eve whispered, careful not to be overheard.

Another office worker came into the room carrying a pile of papers, and Sylvie fidgeted in her seat as they heard voices in the corridor. She turned sideways to look at the door. At that moment it opened, and a tall man with thinning brown hair walked in. He was wearing a pair of corduroy pants and a cardigan over a checked shirt, unbuttoned at the neck. Eve thought he looked a bit like the geography teacher from her senior school, but with eyes like her mother's.

"Welcome to *La Ganterie Dupuis.*" He put out his hand. "Come into my office, *Mesdemoiselles.* I'd like to discuss the terms of your employment. Celeste, would you please bring us some refreshments," he said, turning to the woman who was hovering outside the door.

He switched on his desk lamp, at the same time scratching his head as if he'd forgotten something.

"Now tell me, which one of you two is my niece?" He looked first at Eve and then at Sylvie. Then he winked theatrically at Eve. "Just kidding!"

She went into his arms and he kissed her on both cheeks.

"*Bonjour, Tonton,* I'm so happy to see you after all these years. If *Maman* knew I was here, I know that she would want me to give you her love. This is my friend Sylvie. We're ready to get started, but first we'll need you to find us a radio."

"Whoa... You don't waste any time, do you? No pleasantries? Can't I just chat with my niece for a moment? I need to know more about what's going on in your life."

Celeste lumbered into the room with a tray of mineral water and glasses. Panting slightly, she placed the tray on the desk.

"I think the first thing we must do is get you settled into your lodgings, and then tomorrow morning you can start work," Bertrand said. "I really need skilled workers right now. I don't have the time to train anyone." He noticed that his secretary was listening intently.

"Monsieur, I can take over the interview from here," she said. "No need for you to bother yourself with these two."

"No, I can manage perfectly well—that will be all, Celeste," he said. "Thank you for the water."

"Hmph! Very well, if you say so." Celeste closed the door behind her with a slam.

Bertrand put his finger to his lips, indicating that he wanted the girls to remain silent. Eve could hear Celeste breathing on the other side of the door.

"She's always been a nosy old thing," he whispered. "It's important to keep your identities a secret even from her." He carried on talking about the job offer, until he heard Celeste's footsteps retreating down the corridor.

"I can't believe how much you look like your mother when she was young, although she was not quite so petite. I would have known you anywhere. I hope I am the only one who can recognize the likeness."

"You really don't think anyone will recognize me, do you? I haven't been here since I was a little girl."

"Your mother has been gone a long time. You've changed a lot since you were last here, too. Don't worry about it. Everyone has far more to worry about these days. How is my sister?"

"*Maman* is well. I haven't seen her for nearly two months, but when I left home, she was busy making gloves for the British forces. Have you heard anything from my cousin Olivier? You wrote to say that he has gone into hiding."

"I don't know where he is—I just hope he's safe. None of my contacts have been able to locate him. I pray for him every day." He opened the bottle of water and poured them each a glass.

"I'm so happy you're here. I believe you're crucial to our partisan movement. But first things first—you should get settled into your jobs at the factory. That way you'll spark no unwelcome interest. I hope your mother taught you well—she was an exceptionally talented glovemaker as a young girl."

Eve smiled at her uncle. "I've learned everything I know from her and from Daddy—the two of them make quite the team."

"Good—with you here, I'll be able to give more of my time to the Resistance. Our last radio operator was killed transmitting from a small farmhouse about ten kilometers from here. We don't know who informed on him. It's a huge concern. There are ears and eyes fluttering all over the city. We don't know who to trust anymore. We discovered only the other day that a telephone exchange operator who works here at the exchange on rue Lambert was inadvertently passing messages on to the *Milice*. Her boyfriend is a policeman and she chatted to him about the conversations she overheard each day. Loose gossiping can lose lives very quickly."

Eve turned to Sylvie and frowned as she listened to her

uncle describe the situation.

"But that's not the least of it. The Germans are now able to read the coded messages that our radio operators have been sending. It was my idea to bring you to France to transmit sensitive messages in English code. We really need bilingual speakers."

He picked up his glass and gulped thirstily, before continuing to tell them of his plans.

"But, if you are to work with the partisans, then you must first become invisible. You should simply behave like two young women who are enjoying life in your new home—you have to blend into the background."

"Of course, we've been trained to be discreet," Eve said.

Bertrand lowered himself heavily into his chair, running his hand over his mouth. He looked as if the weight of the war was solely on his shoulders. "It's going to be more difficult now that the Germans are in Grenoble. My wife knows nothing about my work with the Resistance and the Allies. I would like to keep it that way. I wish she could meet you, though."

"We had thought that perhaps we'd be staying with you. I was looking forward to seeing my aunt, but I understand why we can't. Do you know of anywhere we can stay?"

"I have that in hand already. There's a small hostelry in La Place Grenette near the bus terminal. The landlady is very discreet. She won't ask any questions. You should be able to transmit easily from there. I'll walk you over there myself to introduce you."

"Are you sure it's safe to use the radio in the city? We've been instructed only to transmit from the countryside. I'm not sure I like the sound of this," Sylvie said, clenching her fists tightly.

"Don't fret, Sylv, it's all going to be fine. I'm sure Uncle Bertrand knows what's best for us."

"I can assure you that no one will be concerned with two

young women working at the glove factory. You'll be perfectly safe transmitting from your *pension*. However, I can't stress enough that one of you will need to be on the lookout for *les voitures radiogonios*. These are special vehicles that are equipped to detect radios." Bertrand stood up suddenly and slapped his hand on the desk.

"Alright then, let's get going—I'll just let Celeste know that I'm going out." He walked back down the corridor to where Celeste was working.

"How can you be sure that girl is a mechanic? It's not what girls do. Are you sure she's not tricking you?" Celeste asked.

"Why would she trick me? With a severe shortage of qualified mechanics in Grenoble, we're lucky to have found ourselves one. We'll soon find out if she isn't who she says she is, won't we?"

"Well, I should have interviewed them for you, like I always do. How do you know they are properly qualified?"

Celeste liked to be consulted on everything that went on in the factory. As Bertrand's secretary, she placed herself as close to him as she could, feeding him with her views and ideas. After the German invasion of France, she'd made her opinion clear to him that he should cooperate with the Vichy Government and the Italians, and now she'd told him that he should continue to do so with *les Allemandes*.

"I need this job. I have to look after my mother. I'm not lucky enough to have a husband to help me. I hope you know what you're doing."

"We need them, and they've come highly recommended. Don't worry, I still value your opinion. I'm not taking your job away from you. I won't be long. If you can have this typed up by the time I get back, I'd be grateful." Bertrand handed her a piece of paper. "I need you to register the girls' information with the *Mairie*."

They ended up back in La Place Grenette where Monsieur Agard had dropped them earlier that afternoon. Bertrand stopped under the ripped blue awning of the *"Bar-Tabac Duron,"* where tables and chairs were set out in the street. He pointed to a bright green door to the right of the café.

"This is Chez Mimi. She doesn't advertise that she has rooms any longer," he said, "but she's been widowed for many years and likes to take in lodgers to earn a little extra money. I've already checked the place out. There's an escape route through the backyard, should you need it."

He ushered them inside. A brass bell sat on a table in the hallway. He picked it up. The tinkling alerted an elderly lady who shuffled out from behind a thick brocade curtain, a warm smell of baking wafting after her.

"*Bonjour*, Mimi. I've brought the two young ladies I was telling you about. I hope you have their room ready for them."

The old woman was as tiny as a sparrow with gray hair twisted on top of her head in a bun. Flour was sprinkled on her black widow's dress and apron, the whitish dusting giving her an almost ghostly appearance.

"*Alors, Monsieur et les filles*, I've been waiting for you. You've caught me in the middle of baking a walnut bread for your breakfast tomorrow—I was lucky to get my hands on some walnuts the other day. These days we can't let anything go to waste." She twittered on, her bony fingers brushing nervously at her clothes, as she tried to dust off the flour. "Let me show you to your room. If you need dinner tonight, there's a *bistro* on the corner that somehow manages to get fresh meat—no one is sure what it is, though. And Monsieur Duron next door makes a fine omelet if he has the eggs. I can only provide you with breakfast."

Eve resisted the urge to giggle at the woman's chirruping voice and winked at Sylvie. They followed slowly behind her as she struggled up the stairs. When she finally reached the small landing, she went to the second door.

"My bedroom is right next to yours, but I'm hard of hearing, so you won't disturb me at all. If you need to use the toilet, it's outside in the backyard. I'll bring you some water to wash later."

The room, although sparsely furnished with one large bed, a walnut armoire, and one wicker seated chair, had an unobstructed view of the square outside. The window was open, and a fresh smell of beeswax and lavender lingered in the air. A second window overlooked an alleyway at the side of the building.

Bertrand had followed the slow procession up the stairs and was standing on the landing outside their room. "Well, I'll leave you to settle in," he said. "Be at the factory at eight o'clock sharp in the morning." The girls went over to him. He kissed them both on the cheeks before putting his hat back on his head. "I'm very happy you're here," he said with a look that almost resembled relief.

From their window, which overlooked La Place Grenette, there was a view of a fountain. Three soldiers sat on the edge smoking, their guns lying carelessly on the ground. Eve shuddered as she clicked open the lock of her suitcase. The men's presence gave her an unsteady feeling that she had never experienced before. The enemy was now in plain sight and no longer part of her imaginings. On the far side of the square was the bus terminal, where a line of people waited for their transportation home. Outside, under their window, an old man sat cradling a glass of *pastis* at the *bar-tabac*.

She gritted her teeth, trying to shake off the realization that there was no going home. They were here and it was real. "This should be fine. We can see all the comings and goings which will make transmitting easier, and the walls seem thick enough to muffle the noise of the radio receiver. The antenna can go out of this window and should be out of sight from the square. I'll check the escape route later," she said, deliberately trying to sound more purposeful than she actually felt. She lifted the lid of her suitcase. She took out her new folded underwear and stockings and put them in one of the drawers of the armoire.

"Your uncle seems so nice, and luckily you don't look a bit like him," Sylvie said. "I'm not sure about his secretary, though. She seems like a right old battle-axe—did you see the way she looked at us?" she asked.

"You're right. She wasn't very friendly, was she? Maybe she'll lighten up a bit when she gets to know us. I'll butter her up, don't worry!" Eve finished unpacking, sliding her suitcase under the bed. She took off her shoes. "Oh drat, I've got a blister. These shoes have been killing me all day. I wish we'd been given them weeks ago to wear them in."

"My feet are killing me too. They don't look as bad as yours, though." Sylvie yawned.

"Do we still have those sandwiches Madame Duclos gave us?" Eve asked her. "I'm starving."

Sylvie took off her shoes. She'd put her handbag on the only chair in the room. She reached into it and took out the two *baguettes*. "Here," she said, handing Eve the sandwich. "I just want to say I couldn't be here with anyone else except you. Whatever happens, I'll never let you down."

"I know you won't. We're a good team. I'm here for you too. I love you."

"Okay, that's enough soppiness for one day! I need to get some sleep. We've work to do tomorrow." Sylvie turned back the covers on the bed and lay down.

The lavender-scented sheets were cool and soothing, and the pillows surprisingly soft. Within minutes of finishing their sandwiches, they were both fast asleep.

Bright morning light was straining to break through the shutters. A clattering noise coming from the street awakened them. The girls were still fully clothed, not having stirred since the previous evening. Eve cracked open a shutter to see what was going on. Boxes and cartons were being unloaded from trucks in the street right outside their window. Trestle tables were set up in the square where farmers were laying out their meager wares. There were scrawny chickens and rabbits in cages and a few boxes of cabbages and potatoes. It wasn't the same market that it was before the war. Then you could find buckets of cheery flowers, mountains of fresh vegetables, jams, *pâtés,* and hams. Not much food made its way from the country to the city these days, most of it requisitioned at source by the Germans to feed their armies. The clock tower on the other side of the square indicated that it was past six o'clock. Women were already lining up with buckets to get chunks of ice that two young boys were hacking off a large slab with an ice pick. They brought ice down from the mountain twice a week, supplying local bars and restaurants; the remainder they sold at the market. It was the one commodity that was never in short supply.

Just as she was about to close the shutter, a sudden movement made her look out again. A young boy dressed in a shabby coat with a yellow star attached to the sleeve tripped as he ran past one of the ice boys. The eggs that he was carrying smashed to the ground, leaving a bright yellow patch on the cobblestones. The elderly farmer whose eggs he'd stolen was huffing and puffing, as he chased him from the other side of the square. He caught up to the boy and, lifting him off the ground by his arm, smacked him hard across the face. The ice boy standing nearby staggered back in surprise, dropping a large chunk on the ground.

"You dirty little Jew! You stole my eggs. You'll pay for this, you can be sure," the farmer shouted. The man's face was red with anger; spittle from his mouth wobbled on his thick beard. The boy wriggled in his grip and almost got away, but the uproar alerted two German soldiers lounging on the edge of the fountain. Before anyone realized what was happening, one of the soldiers had taken aim at the child with his rifle. A single shot rang out. The boy fell from the farmer's grip. As he hit the cobblestones, dark red blood gushed from his ear and trickled to the ground, mingling with the yellow of the egg yolks and the broken shells. The farmer looked down at the body lying face down on the ground. He froze in shock. The child was dead, but blood kept gushing from where the bullet had penetrated his body. The old man picked the boy up by the shoulders, trying to shake him back to life.

"Can someone help me? Please..." But in the square, everyone stood still, paralyzed with fear.

Eve put her hand over her mouth in horror, unable to speak, silently willing the boy to get up, mesmerized by the sight of the blood flowing from his still body. Visions of Frank in his school uniform floated in front of her eyes, his earnest little freckled face grinning up at her. She struggled to breathe and tasted salty tears trickling into her mouth. She wiped them away with her hand, smearing them over her cheeks and nose. The bed was the only place of comfort. Sylvie grasped the brass frame and sank down heavily next to her on the mattress. Eve didn't even realize she was trembling as she grasped Sylvie's arm. The incident had all taken place in a matter of minutes, but to the girls, it seemed like everything had happened in slow motion. With just one snap of a finger, the child was dead.

They sat, huddled together, unable to move when they heard a feeble tap on their bedroom door.

"Shush!" Eve got up and put her ear to the door. On the other side she could hear Mimi sobbing. "What's wrong with everyone? They've killed little Antoine Dreyfus, the clock-maker's son from rue des Écoles. Monsieur Dreyfus and his wife disappeared last year—no one knew what had become of the boy. He must have been hiding somewhere. That poor little soul."

Eve opened the door just in time to see Mimi crumple in a heap. Kneeling on either side of her, they both put their arms around her. Then they all wept.

Outside in the square, it was quiet. The usual loud banter of the stallholders and the shrill voices of haggling housewives on market day evaporated into terrified whispers. The police arrived within minutes. They summoned the undertaker to remove the child's body to the mortuary. Monsieur Duron came out of the *bar-tabac* next door with a bucket of water to sluice away the gruesome evidence of the child's death. His face scrunched up with a look of pain as he carried out the task, unable to look down at the cobblestones. People shuffled around, their eyes downcast, going about their business. The farmer knelt near the place where the boy had fallen, holding his head in his hands, weeping. The bell in the clock tower rang once for the half hour. It was still only six-thirty.

"Oh my God, I can't believe what just happened. He was a child—he looked just like our Frankie. Who kills children? He must have been starving. Why didn't the man let him have the eggs? He'd only stolen eggs!" Color drained from Eve's face as she stared at Sylvie in despair.

"I don't know," Sylvie said. "But now I understand when they told us we won't know who our enemy is. They're fighting with each other, as well as with the Germans."

CHAPTER 10

GEORGINA AND EVE
Worcester, 2016

Georgina sat curled up in the comfy armchair that Eve kept in her bedroom for visitors. She listened in dismay to what Eve was telling her.

"I realized then that there is no black and white in the world, just lots of muddy areas in between, where people make their own justice, and that the instinct to survive is primeval," Eve said. "My only previous experience of war was learned from the cinema: propaganda films put out by The Ministry of Information encouraging everyone to band together, to do their bit. I was so naïve. I had silly romantic notions that if we did the right thing, we could save everyone. I learned quickly that war is much more complicated than that. The realization hit me hard. But I so wanted to stop what was happening. Evil like that has no place in the world."

Georgina stood up and paced back and forth, her hands thrust into the pockets of her skinny jeans. She pulled her hair back tightly from her face, tying it in a ponytail.

"Oh, Grandy! I feel as if I was there too. It's awful."

"I wanted to protect that little boy—but I couldn't. He was the first dead body I ever saw. They didn't teach us how to cope with that in training. Once I witnessed the horror of him being killed, I was never able to unsee it. He was the same age as Frankie. It was as if he didn't matter. The picture in my mind of the market that morning will always be there."

"But you weren't a soldier, and you were so young. Couldn't you have come home after that?" Georgina took out a tissue from her pocket to blot the tears that were brimming in her eyes.

"No, that was never on the cards. It was just the beginning of our mission. I was so determined to help thwart the German's advance in whatever way I could. I'm sorry—it must be difficult for you to hear. I understand that. I've buried everything deep inside me for years. I had the most intense need to survive most of the time, but some days I could have put my hands in the air and let them shoot me. It's not easy to understand the thin line between hope and despair. I've never returned to France, you know."

"Why didn't you tell your parents what happened to you when you got back?"

"I'd signed the Official Secrets Act. They taught us to keep secrets. I couldn't tell anyone. I wanted to forget—I came home and got on with my life as best I could. It's what we all did back then. There was no choice but to hide behind the lies, and I thought that somehow gave me a shell to protect myself with. But now I realize there is no escape from what happened, and I dream about it all the time." Eve closed her eyes and grasped the coverlet in her hands.

"You're exhausted." Georgina sat down on the edge of the bed. She stroked her grandmother's hand as if she was soothing a child. "We can carry on with your story some other time when you feel up to it. I haven't been feeling very well all day. It must be something I ate yesterday. I think we both need a break. Can I get you something to drink?"

"Yes, I think I would like something. Perhaps a small glass of sherry might help me relax. You look after yourself and get some rest too." Her head sank back against the pillow. Georgina kissed her grandmother on the forehead, fussing motherly with her bedcovers.

Downstairs, light from the streetlamp outside the house was flickering into the dark living room, making shadows on the carpet. Just feet from the window, a group of teenagers were jostling and shoving each other as they moved along the pavement, grunting and swearing as they went by. Eileen stood in the open doorway.

"Oi!" she shouted after the youngsters. "How many times have I told you lot not to drop your fish and chip wrappers on my doorstep. Pick them up. There's a perfectly good dustbin at the end of the street."

She watched as one of the teenagers turned back to look at her and stuck up two fingers. She slammed the door shut in disgust, the dirty papers in her hand. "Bloody kids. I don't know what their parents teach them these days, but it isn't manners..."

Georgina laughed. She'd never heard Eileen quite so angry or animated before.

Eileen returned to the kitchen to prepare a tray for Eve's dinner. Taking a plate out of the warming drawer, she dished out a lamb chop along with Brussels sprouts and mashed potatoes. She had already taken a bottle of white wine out of the fridge, and two glasses from the cupboard for herself and Georgina.

"My grandmother is quite remarkable. She's been telling me about her life as a young woman during World War Two." She found the sherry in a cupboard.

"I like your grandmother a lot. I can tell she's a tough old thing. She hasn't told me anything about her experiences, but I know she's from a generation that suffered a lot. My mother lost her older brother in the War. She never got over it." She picked up the tray and handed it to Georgina. "Now be a dear and take this up to her, would you?"

Georgina took the tray from her. Halfway out of the door she turned back. "I'm really not very hungry, but do you mind if I sit with you while you eat? Don't pour any wine for me. I've got a bit of a headache. I'll take this up to Grandy now."

Upstairs, Georgina found that Eve had already nodded off to sleep. Leaving the glass of sherry on the bedside table, Georgina took the tray back downstairs. She put the plate in the oven to keep warm for later. Eileen was sitting at the island, reading something on her phone. She glanced up at Georgina.

"Isn't she hungry?"

"She was fast asleep." Georgina sat down. "You've never told me about your family. Do you have any children?"

"Yes. I've got two teenage girls. That's a challenge, I can tell you. They're fourteen and sixteen going on twenty and twenty-five. When I get a job like this, they stay with my sister. My husband died five years ago."

"I'm sorry. That must be awful for you. How in the world do you manage to do it all? I know what you do here for my grandmother, and that's enough."

"Didn't I tell you? I was a juggler in the circus in my last job!" Even though she was grinning, her eyes unexpectedly filled with tears. "Seriously though, I'm lucky to have a wonderful family who supports me. They've all pitched in since Dave died. I couldn't manage without them."

"Thank you for all you do for her. I could never do what you do for a stranger. I can just about manage to look after myself."

"That's not true. I've seen how good you are with your grandmother. She's perked up so much since you arrived. The doctor was very concerned about her."

Rain was pouring down when Georgina met up with Camilla in the town center a few days later. They discovered a coffee shop in the precinct that they both liked. It was the only place Georgina was able to find a double mocha latte that was up to her New York standards.

Georgina looked absent-mindedly at the passersby outside the window.

"Remember we used to do this when we were young?"

"What, have coffee together?"

"No. Looking at strangers and trying to guess who they are, where they come from, where they're going. I always loved that game."

"Is everything alright?" Camilla asked. "You seem a bit down in the dumps."

Georgina fiddled nervously with a packet of sugar. The contents spilled over the table. She groaned.

"I don't know if I want to say this out loud—but here goes. I've been feeling funny for a few days. Just queasy and stuff. I took a pregnancy test last night. It's positive."

Camilla grabbed hold of her hand. "Oh, my goodness. How are you feeling? What are you going to do? Who's the father?"

"Whoa, slow down. I'm just getting my head around it, and now I've said the words, it's real... I think I'm going to throw up again. How long does this nausea last for?" The color drained from Georgina's face.

Camilla opened and closed her mouth. She took an almond biscotti from a paper bag on the table. "Eat this," she said, handing it to Georgina. "It usually only lasts for the first couple of months. Dry biscuits help. Who's the father?" she asked again.

"I'm pretty sure it's Marco. He's really the only guy I've slept with recently, although there was someone when I went to Mexico at the end of February..."

"Marco? Why have you never told me about him?"

Georgina crunched down hard on the biscotti. "Well, you know me. I never take anything seriously, but it got complicated when he wanted to introduce me to his mother. We had a row just before I left, and I haven't heard from him since."

"Oh, Georgie." Camilla ran her fingers through her hair and sighed.

"I didn't plan on getting pregnant," Georgina said. "I don't know what went wrong with my birth control. I like him, but I don't want a serious relationship with him."

"Is that why you thought meeting his mother would complicate things?"

"Yes, that, and one of my friends said he could be after my money. It had me thinking."

"Why would you think he is?"

"Well, he doesn't have any, for one thing. He's a writer who works as a part-time waiter at the Plaza Grand. We've just been having fun."

"What are you going to do?"

"I really don't know."

"Well, there are options. And you certainly don't need to marry him."

"Marry him! I don't want to get married to anyone right now. And can you imagine what Mum would say? She would probably have a fit if I told her I was going to marry a waiter from the Bronx."

"Have you told your grandmother?"

"No, I wanted to talk things through with you first. Grandy had to marry someone she didn't want to because she came back from France pregnant. It ruined everyone's life, so I think

I know what she'll say."

"Lots of people are single parents now."

"Should I tell him?"

"Well, he does have the right to know. It's his child too."

"Yes, he does. I'm sure at his stage in life he doesn't want a kid, though."

"What's he like? Would I like him?"

"Well, he's nice. I don't think marriage material though. There's a definite spark between us. But I don't love him. Anyway, he thinks I'm a rich bitch, and that's why I haven't heard from him. I don't know. Everything in my life is so random. All my relationships have been hit or miss. What can I say? I've always liked it like that until now. I feel if I try to make something happen, I'll screw up. And my family doesn't exactly have a good track record with relationships. When I look at you and Matt, I'm starting to think something is wrong with me. Why can't I find someone to love?"

"You will one day. When you know, you know."

"Grandy said that too. Step by step. I'm going to see a doctor. Do you think I should worry Grandy about it?"

"Well, she's a wise old bird. You need your family around you. What do you think your mother is going to say?"

"Knowing her, she'll be pissed."

"OK. Let's take it one day at a time. I'll look after you. I'm glad you're here. Do you think you want to keep the baby? It's a huge commitment, especially without a partner."

"I know. I want to keep it. But I could really use your help. I'm going to make a hopeless mother." Georgina's eyes welled up with tears.

"Of course you're not. Everyone worries about that. Look how you're taking care of your grandmother." Camilla gave her friend a reassuring smile. "Sorry to change the subject, but do you remember Matt's friend is visiting from London at the weekend? Do you still want to come?"

"I haven't turned into a pumpkin or something just

because I'm pregnant. But I can't on Saturday night. Eileen is going home to see her family. Could I come for Sunday lunch instead?"

"Absolutely. I'll do a roast—I'm sure you haven't had one for years—all the trimmings." She reached over and squeezed Georgina's hand. "It's going to be okay."

"I'm not ready to tell anyone else about this just yet," Georgina said. "Please don't tell Matt."

Camilla put her hand over her heart. "You have my word."

CHAPTER 11

EVE AND SYLVIE
France, 1943

The last thing the girls wanted to do was go to work after what they had witnessed, but they dressed and went downstairs in search of Mimi. They found her in the kitchen where she put out three bowls on a pitch pine table. They sat down, watching the old lady fuss about heating milk that had boiled over earlier. The girls noticed that her hands were shaking as she tried to pour what was left of the contents of the pan into the bowls. Eve finally got up to help her.

"Let me do that—sit down. Where's the coffee?"

Mimi pointed to a white enamel pot on the stove.

Eve poured them each some coffee. The bitter smell of burnt milk hung in the air like a damp cloud in the small kitchen, making her nauseous. Bile rose in her throat. She swallowed hard. The walnut bread sat on a wooden board in the middle of the table, waiting to be cut.

"I'm sorry, Mimi, but I couldn't eat a thing right now." She rushed from the room, just reaching the outhouse in time before she retched.

When they finally ventured out, they found the square empty except for a few remaining stalls, where vendors were loading up their boxes into trucks. Among them was the farmer who had initiated the atrocity. He dragged his feet now, as if he was aware of the feeling of revulsion surrounding him. People he knew shunned him; some even spat on the ground as he walked by.

It was warm for seven forty-five in the morning, but most of the regular shoppers had already gone home. Two soldiers dressed in the black uniform of the Waffen-SS were sitting at the *bar-tabac* next door. Monsieur Duron arrived with a bottle of *cognac* and two glasses. He slammed them down on the table. One of the men lit a cigarette, snapping his fingers to indicate that he wanted an ashtray. The bar owner picked one up from an adjoining table and tossed it in front of him without acknowledging him. The older of the two men took off his cap. He threw it casually on the table, swinging his foot up to follow it. Reaching for the bottle, he poured himself an inch of brandy, knocking it back in one go. And then he poured another. The table sat between the girls and the street. If they'd wanted to, they could have touched the enemy. The officer turned and looked them up and down.

"What do we have here? Don't worry, we don't bite little girls like you." He snapped his yellow teeth together like a shark and laughed menacingly. The smell of alcohol floated from his breath into the chilly morning air, making Eve feel like she might throw up again. In the end, it was Sylvie who took the lead.

She gripped Eve by the hand. Without looking back at the men, she marched purposefully into the street. "Bastard," she muttered under her breath when they were out of earshot.

Bertrand was outside the factory door pacing back and forth when they arrived for work.

"I heard what happened this morning," he said. "I hope you didn't witness the shooting."

"We saw it all—that poor child. It was horrific." Eve's lip quivered, her eyes glistening with tears. Sylvie, still holding her hand, nodded her head in agreement.

Coming up behind them, Celeste struggled for breath as she labored up the three steps leading to the front door. "Are you talking about the Jewish boy who was killed this morning? If you ask me, he deserved what he got. He shouldn't have been stealing. There isn't enough food to go around, without letting Jews take it from us." She stood up straight and stuck out her chest importantly.

Eve stared at the woman with her mouth wide open and gripped Sylvie's hand even tighter.

"That's enough, Celeste—please get to work," Bertrand snapped at her. He watched as she flung the door open, letting it slam behind her. "That woman! I don't know what's got into her lately. If she hadn't worked here for so long and wasn't so trustworthy, I'd have her out of here in a heartbeat. I'm sorry that you must start your work here under such a cloud. Let me show you around. It may take your mind off things."

The main floor of the factory was well equipped and spacious, with a lofted ceiling and efficient industrial lighting. Large metal worktables were set in the center of the room, rolls of leather propped up against one long wall.

"Over there you'll find the tanned skins. The Germans have sold us mainly cowhide and pigskin, but you'll find some goatskin too. Unfortunately, they don't pay us the going rate for our finished product and we're operating at a loss. We don't make many gloves for the retail business any longer. When the Vichy government made a deal with the Germans, we lost our autonomy. Now *les Boches* are in control, I can see we are going to be doing their bidding."

"This is a much bigger factory than my parents'. You must have had a large operation at one time, judging by all your equipment. What's behind that door?" Eve pointed to a heavy metal door marked with a red cross.

"That's the dye room. For safety reasons we always keep it locked. We're down to seven employees now—this is Marie, my head cutter, and Sandrine, who oversees preparing the gloves for stitching." He nodded his head towards two women dressed in dark blue overalls who were sharing a cigarette before they started work. They gave Eve and Sylvie a little wave. "Over there's old Herbert, who has maintained the machinery for years, but it's getting too much for him. Sylvie, I'd like you to take over from him. Many of our workers have disappeared. Some were Jews who were taken to work camps, and others young men who have gone into hiding or been imprisoned by the authorities."

There were four other women, two operating sewing machines, one ironing the already-stitched gloves, and one lining them with what looked like fleece inserts.

"The shaped gloves have traditionally been taken out to workers in villages outside Grenoble, who then stitch them and turn them. The Germans are demanding a special lining, which is delaying things. It hasn't been easy to maintain a steady production, but we're doing the best we can."

"How many gloves do you make each month?" Eve asked. The stock on the shelves looked extremely low.

"We've been lucky until now that the Vichy government didn't put too high a demand on us. But the Nazis have told us to increase our production to one hundred pairs a week—just for their armies. As I said, we won't see much of a profit, and it's going to be an impossible task given our lack of personnel. I'm not even sure how I will pay those I have..."

"That's why we're here to help. Let's get started and see how we can increase production for you," Eve said confidently. She picked up a roll of leather and tossed it over her shoulder. "I'll help Marie by stretching the leather, if she does the cutting." Putting the roll down on the table, she took off her cardigan. She picked up a faded cotton overall that had been hanging on a chair.

Time passed quickly as she found herself in a familiar rhythm. She worked alongside the head cutter, who was singing as she worked, turning out the cut glove shapes quickly and efficiently.

"Where did you learn to cut out gloves like that?"

"My mother taught me. Her family are all *Grenoblois* and have always been in the glove-making business. But it's not what I really want to do with my life," Marie said. She chewed on her lip, concentrating on her task. The heavy industrial scissors looked huge in her small hands as she exacted a new cut in the leather.

"*Maman* taught me too. My family are glovemakers in Paris. But what would you rather be doing?"

"There's a small nightclub on La rue Rivoli where I perform a couple of times a month. It's a hole in the wall, but a fun place to go. Perhaps you can come to hear me sing later this week." Marie took a cigarette out of a tortoiseshell holder and lit it, offering the case to Eve. Eve shook her head.

"I hope I'll be able to keep singing, but German soldiers have started going there lately and the atmosphere has changed."

Later, during their lunch break, the women were sitting on the wall overlooking the river. The fast-flowing water rushed past them. It was surprisingly hot for an overcast day. Eve dangled her hand in the icy water, then patted her temples with her fingers.

"I know now isn't the time for me to launch a singing career—I just earn a few extra francs when I can. I'm trying to get my name out there. Maybe when the war is over, I'll become famous," Marie said.

"I've never heard anyone with a voice like yours. I'd love to come and hear you," Sylvie said. "You should hear Eve sing. It's like listening to a catfight. Perhaps you can give her a few tips!"

"Very funny! I thought you were my friend," Eve said, flicking water in Sylvie's face. "It'll be fun to get out and see the local nightlife. *Maman* always told me the men from Grenoble are good-looking. I can't wait to see for myself."

"Don't expect too much after Paris. I'm sure your standards are much higher. Anyway, most of the good ones are taken or have left already."

"Oh, we're not too fussy. We just want to have some fun. Isn't that right, Sylvie?"

"Yes, we do, but I really want to hear you sing," she said earnestly. Her eyes locked with Marie's momentarily. Eve noticed that Sylvie was blushing.

"Good. It's a date then. I'll buy you both a drink," Marie said.

Following the sound of blaring music, Eve and Sylvie easily found the nightclub. Locals and German soldiers were spilling out onto the street. Inside, they saw Marie alone at the bar. She gripped onto the bar stool as if it was a life raft, looking terrified of what would happen if she were to let go in the sea of soldiers. They fought their way through the crowd to get to her.

"What are you going to have to drink? It's on me," Marie said, her body now visibly relaxing, her hands reaching out to welcome them.

"I don't know. I'm not much of a drinker. The last drink I had was cider at Christmas. What are you drinking?" Eve asked.

"I thought you *Parisiennes* would be a bit more sophisticated than that. Try it—it's *Vermouth Cassis*. It's made with sweet vermouth mixed with blackcurrant liqueur and soda water. It's not strong."

Sylvie leaned over and took a sip from Marie's glass. "Yum—that's delicious. Have some, Eve."

Eve tasted the drink and nodded her head in agreement. The elderly barman took his time mixing their drinks.

"Marie shouldn't have brought you here. There are too many drunken *Allemandes* hanging around," he whispered through the side of his mouth, pushing their drinks towards them. He turned his back, rearranging his bottles, but still taking surreptitious glances at what was going on in the mirror that backed the bar.

Eve recognized the soldier who shot the little boy earlier that week. He was young, probably eighteen or nineteen, and in different times was someone she wouldn't even notice. But now his face was stamped in her memory. Her chest boiled with anger. He smiled at her. She stirred her drink with the cocktail stick and looked away. She touched Sylvie on the arm and put her head close to hers. "Talk to me about something, anything. Just don't let that bastard near us."

Their drinks slipped down easily, and Sylvie ordered another round. They started to relax. Marie and Sylvie became more animated as they chatted away with each other. Eve noticed a spark between them and was happy that Sylvie had found a friend. It was good to mix with the locals—the more friends they made, the easier it would be to blend in.

After half an hour, the lights were dimmed. Marie finished her drink, leaving the girls at the bar. Minutes later they watched as she stepped onto the stage. She had changed into a shimmery cocktail dress that hugged her perfectly proportioned figure. She wore no makeup on her face except a splash of bright scarlet lipstick. She settled in the circle of a downlight. The rest of the room was in darkness, the silence charged with a hum of anticipation from the crowd. The pianist struck the first chords of a well-known song, and cradling the microphone in two hands, Marie started to sing. The humming stopped. All that could be heard was her husky, sensual voice echoing off the stone walls. Everyone stood transfixed by her illuminated figure. When she finished, the light slowly faded. She stood in the darkness listening to the cheers and whistling, as everyone clapped boisterously, shouting for an encore. As she took her final bow, a soldier staggered onto the stage, lunging at her. She stumbled forward on her high heels, plunging into the darkness of the nightclub.

She tried to pick herself off the ground, but a soldier grabbed her. He groped her with his hands, violating her body, before tossing her to a comrade, as if they were playing a game of 'pass the parcel'. Some minutes passed before someone switched the lights back on, revealing Marie on the floor; the bodice of her dress was ripped open, exposing her underwear, her lipstick smeared like blood across her face. Eve grabbed Sylvie to restrain her, but she pulled her arm out of Eve's grip.

As Eve watched Sylvie make her way across the room, a shot rang out. A Gestapo officer stood in the center of the room with a gun in his hand. Sylvie put her hands in the air with a terrified look on her face.

"This is not how young men of the Fatherland should behave. This young lady has just entertained you. I expect you to treat her with respect." The officer spoke in German, holding his pistol in the air in a threatening manner. A hush fell over the room and the soldiers fell back, leaving Marie on the ground. The stocky German lunged towards her, pushing the men out of his way; a gold tooth glinted in his mouth as he snarled at the men, his face growing red with anger and excitement. He had removed his cap. His head was shiny and almost completely bald except for a few stringy strands of hair that he had combed pathetically across his scalp.

"Let me escort you home," he said in French. Helping her to her feet he took off his jacket and placed it over her shoulders in a supposedly gallant gesture. "I apologize for the men's disgraceful behavior."

Marie whimpered. She pulled his jacket tightly around her shoulders, using it to cover her torn dress, nervously touching the insignia on its lapel with her fingers. The officer put his arm around her waist. In the dim light of the room, Eve could see that Marie's eyes were darting around frantically, as if she was looking for her friends. She watched as the officer half supported and half dragged Marie towards the door.

"Let's go. I have to stop him." Sylvie started after them.

Eve gripped Sylvie's forearm and held her back. "Don't—there's nothing we can do. We can't bring ourselves to his attention. I can tell he's a dangerous man."

His eyes shone with excitement as if he had just won a prize. Sylvie stared after them, her eyes scorching the man's back with hatred.

The girls were relieved to see Marie at work on Monday morning, but what they saw confirmed their worst fears.

"Oh my God—what did he do to you?" Eve banged her fist on the worktable.

"Your poor mouth! And what's the scarf hiding?" Sylvie gently removed the silk square from Marie's neck to reveal ugly blue and black markings that matched the ones on her face. "I swear I am going to make that bastard pay—I could kill him!"

"I thought he was going to take me home. But he took me back to his room in the Hotel de Grenoble." Marie's lip was so badly split she was barely able to speak. "No way to escape... I tried to fight him off..."

Eve was slightly surprised by the tenderness in Sylvie's eyes as her friend put her arm around Marie's shoulders, hugging her close. It was a vulnerability in Sylvie's tough shell that she'd never seen before.

Bertrand was pacing back and forth in his office. Eve had never seen him look so pinched and gray. His hands moved up and down, gesticulating angrily. "I know you want to get your claws into Marie's attacker. I'm just as mad as you are, but he's an important man and we can't report him to the police. He *is* the police. Right now, though, more important things must take precedence over your friend."

"What is more important than getting revenge for Marie?" Sylvie asked. "I am so angry right now I could strangle him with my bare hands."

"I know, I know, but we have to stay calm and there's work to be done," said Bertrand. "Your radio has finally arrived. It was part of a drop last night, and an agent will deliver it to you this evening. Plan on getting back to your lodgings by five-thirty. When you've set up the radio later tonight, I have some urgent messages that I need you to transmit to England. M19 has informed us that they have British pilots that need to be picked up. They're in hiding somewhere safe for now. We must organize the pick-up this week at the airstrip near Vassieux. If you receive a return message from London, Eve, you'll take it to Saint-Nizier-du-Moucherotte tomorrow. It's a small village about eight kilometers outside the city. I'll try to find transport for you. There's an agent there who will pass the message on through the correct network."

"What's the name of the agent who's delivering the radio?" Eve asked.

Sylvie wasn't paying any attention and was still pacing back and forth. She had a determined look on her face like a lion hunting its prey.

"Jules, and he'll be carrying the radio in a suitcase. He'll pretend he is looking for somewhere to stay. Don't worry about Mimi. She won't say a word."

"We'll be there." Eve took Sylvie's hand. "Come on, Sylv, let's go for a walk for five minutes. You need some fresh air." She had never seen her friend so rattled before.

Celeste was hovering in the corridor when they came out of Bertrand's office. "What have you two been talking to Monsieur Dupuis about? Is it about Marie? Flaunting herself in front of men—what a tramp! I hear you two were there too."

"What a nasty thing to say! You have no idea what happened—Marie did no such thing," Sylvie said sharply. "Unfortunately, Monsieur Dupuis has informed us that there is no point in going to the police. The officer who committed the crime holds the highest position in the city—he's Gruppenführer Müller, the Head of the Gestapo. But I swear I will get him back one day."

The next morning, Eve set off with the message on a shaky bicycle that her Uncle Bertrand found for her. He'd attached a wicker basket to the front handlebars and a larger one at the back, where she put the brown paper parcel of gloves and two glove forms. Earlier she'd memorized the detailed directions he'd given her for the route she was to take. It was more difficult now to pass over the bridge each day to work, as German soldiers had started making spot checks all over the city. She was glad that she'd be leaving the city on a much smaller road, where, she hoped, checkpoints had yet to be set up. Her identity papers were safely tucked into her bag, which she slung across her body.

The autumn sun was lower in the sky, leaving the summer heat behind, but its glare was still dazzling, and she pulled down the broad brim of her felt hat to keep it from shining in her eyes. The road proved to be easy going for the first ten minutes, as she left the outskirts of Grenoble, but gradually it started to climb steeply; the surface changed to rough gravel, making pedaling difficult, and the bicycle wobbled precariously. Out of breath, she dismounted, pushing the bike instead. Still panting heavily, she stopped again to take off her cardigan. Underneath she wore a short-sleeved white cotton blouse, sprigged with tiny violet flowers. Inhaling scents of lavender and thyme, she tied her cardigan around her waist, thinking that she was glad of the rigorous training she had undergone in Scotland. On one side of the road, the land sloped away to a sunburnt valley, where a snaking river glistened in the sunlight. Two farm workers were methodically forking piles of hay into ricks to dry, working across the field in an age-old rhythm that was almost musical. A sheepdog ran around and around in circles, playing in the falling hay, while a hawk swooped down from the sky, its sharp eyes locating a mouse trying to hide in the stubble. Catching the creature in its beak, it flew off to devour its prey.

The view on the other side of the track was completely different. A thick tapestry of yellow, green, and gold foliage glowed in the sun; the leaves of beech, oak, and Norway maple trees were changing their colors as summer slowly faded away. Birds were flying from branch to branch, dipping and diving to catch flies in the morning air. The sunshine sparkled through the leaves, casting dancing shadows on the ground, the silence of the morning intermittently broken by echoes of woodpeckers drilling for insects in the woods. The warm breeze tickled her face, and lifting her hands above her head, she gazed about her in wonder. It seemed unfair that she was able to enjoy such a perfect day when there was so much suffering in the city.

She continued climbing, pushing her bike for about half an hour, when she heard frantic barking coming from the woods. Trees now bordered the road on both sides; she had no idea where the noise was coming from. A large dog appeared from a gap in the trees to her right. It raced towards her, barking furiously, followed by a young man carrying a stick.

"Milou, Milou. Get down!" the man shouted. The dog had reached Eve's side and was jumping playfully.

"I'm so sorry—I don't know what got into him," the man said. "He's usually so obedient. One minute he was chasing a rabbit, then he just disappeared. Don't worry, he won't hurt you—I think he likes you."

But Eve didn't like him. A dog had bitten her when she was a child, and this one, with its slavering mouth and muscular body, brought back memories that made her shudder. She gripped the handlebars of the bicycle tightly, her knuckles turning white. She started off again, the gravel of the rough road crunching under her feet, trying her best to ignore the lively dog and its master. She had only gone a few yards when she heard the man following her. He caught up to her with the German Shepherd now restrained by a piece of rope.

"I haven't seen you around here before—where are you going?"

She dithered about answering him, before finally deciding that it couldn't do any harm.

"I'm delivering gloves to Madame Corot for her to stitch. I'm a glovemaker in the city."

"Well, you're almost there—Madame Corot's house is around the next bend. It's at the edge of the village next to the graveyard beyond the stone wall. I didn't know she took in work—I suppose she must need to now. Do you mind if I walk

124

along with you? I'm going that way."

"Well, I can't stop you. Besides, I don't think I can ride my bike up that hill."

"I'm Luc," he said, offering her his hand. He chattered on pleasantly. "I'm staying with my father on our farm about a mile from here. He hasn't been very well. I've been helping him get the hay in for winter—I'm usually at university."

"Shouldn't you be working in Germany?" Eve asked.

"My professor signed papers early on confirming that I'm a student at the university. The Nazis haven't bothered me yet, but I'm sure they'll come to get me one day soon. Papa thinks I should go into hiding—but I can't leave him. *Maman* died a few years ago."

"I'm Eve Charlot. I came here from Paris with my friend Sylvie. We thought that we were escaping the German occupation by coming to the Free Zone, but now the Germans are here too. There's no getting away from them."

As he walked alongside her, she was able to study him more closely. He towered over her, with broad shoulders that accentuated his athletic body. Everything was different about him; he looked nothing like the British boys Eve was used to back home, with their short back and side hairstyles and smooth faces. He had blonde hair that hung almost to his chin, while the darker hair of his stubbly beard gave him a strong and rugged appearance. His deep blue eyes reminded her of the sea on a summer's day. There was something about him that made her want to keep looking. As she shamelessly gazed at him, a sudden gust of wind whipped her hair into her eyes, and she took off her hat to scrape it back into place. As she did so, the bicycle wobbled and fell to the ground, the pedal gouging her leg.

"Are you okay?" He knelt beside her and let go of the dog.

"Oh, it's nothing," she said weakly. She touched her leg and winced. She watched as blood from the cut oozed down into her white ankle sock. Reaching into his pocket, Luc took out a large handkerchief. He expertly pressed it against the wound to stem the bleeding.

"It's quite a deep gash—let me take care of it."

A warm breeze caressed her face. His fingers touched her leg, making her heart stop momentarily. Everything seemed to be happening in slow motion and she felt a tingle shoot through her body. Looking up at Luc's face, she realized that he too felt the energy that passed between them. The tenderness in his eyes, and his breath on her bare arm as he cleaned the cut, felt exquisitely intimate. It was as if she had known him her whole life, that he was already a part of her, like she'd come home. She trembled. As he wrapped his handkerchief around her leg, his face hovered alarmingly close to hers, his lips tantalizingly near. Her desire to kiss his mouth was so strong that she almost did.

"You should get that cleaned up later with some anti-septic—you don't want it to get infected. It shouldn't need stitches though," he said, breaking her trance. "Are you sure you're okay? You look a little pale and you're shivering. Do you think you'll be able to ride your bicycle?"

She took a deep breath, enjoying the warmth of his touch as he held her hand. "I think I'll be alright in a moment. Thank you," she said, desperately trying to regain her composure. But try as she might, she couldn't; the pain in her leg was nothing compared to the effect he was having on her heart. She stared at his face, memorizing every tiny detail, as if nothing else mattered. She reluctantly tore her eyes away from him, her sense of propriety finally taking charge. "I really should get going if Madame Corot is to get the gloves stitched by next week. You've been so kind."

She noticed that the confidence that Luc had while tending to her leg seemed to have vanished. He knelt next to her, still holding her hand, squeezing it nervously. He opened his mouth to say something, but no words came out.

"Do you come here often?" he eventually blurted out.

She laughed. "I'll be back next week to pick up the gloves. Perhaps we can meet again then."

"Yes. I'd really like that." He let go of her hand.

Beaming broadly, he reached down to right her bicycle. As they slowly walked along, he kept sneaking a look at her. A climbing rose was growing along the wall bordering Madame Corot's house. He stopped to pick one of the deep pink flowers. As he handed it to her, their fingers touched and the same sparks she'd felt earlier crackled up her arm and a yearning quivered deep inside her belly.

It was Madame Corot who broke the spell. She came out of her *chalet*, shooing away a couple of hens that were rummaging through her vegetables, making them protest noisily. Rows of cabbages, potatoes, and beans had long since replaced her perennial gardens, although a few of her precious sunflowers and hollyhocks had seeded themselves in between the straight lines. The branches of an apple tree, heavy with fruit, hung over the garden gate, almost blocking the entrance.

"Would you like one?" she asked, ducking under the tree to open the gate.

"It's been a really good crop this year. It must have been all the rain we had in the spring." She picked an apple and handed it to Eve. "But my chickens have stopped laying," she said.

"How many hens do you keep?" Eve waited for her response.

"Just four these days," the woman replied, giving the correct password.

She turned to Luc. "*Bonjour, jeune homme.* How's your papa?"

"He's fine, thank you. I should really get going," he said, turning to look at Eve one last time. "Until next week."

"I see you met Luc Gaspard. He's a good boy helping his papa. He's going to be a doctor, you know—he's quite the catch. Most of the girls in the village are after him," the young

127

widow said, pushing a strand of blonde hair out of her eyes.

She smoothed her hands down the sides of her black dress. Losing her husband at thirty-five had been hard. Stitching gloves was her only source of income. Helping the Resistance, though, was something that she was doing to avenge Paul's death.

"I didn't know he's studying to be a doctor," Eve replied. She buried her nose in the rose he had given her. She felt her face go red as she stared longingly after him.

"That must be why he has such a gentle touch. He fixed my leg," she said wistfully.

"Do you have something for me, *Mademoiselle*?" Madame Corot asked a little impatiently.

"Yes. I'm sorry. Here are the gloves, and these messages are for you to pass on to your contact. Please don't read them—just hand them over. The less you know, the better. I will be back next week to pick up the gloves. Do you have anything for me to take back to Grenoble?"

"Jules delivered a note to me this morning. The information needs to be transmitted to London as soon as possible." She fished for a folded piece of paper in her apron pocket and handed it to Eve.

Without reading the note, Eve took the glove form that was sitting in the back basket of her bicycle and stuffed it into one of the fingers. The sound of a child crying made her look around. Madame Corot had already turned her back on her and was walking back to the house, waving her hand as she went.

"I have to go. *À bientôt.*"

"*Au revoir, Madame.* I'll see you next week."

She set off, limping slightly. Although her leg was smarting badly and her sock probably ruined, she couldn't help but think that she would remember this day for the rest of her life. A huge smile lit up her face.

CHAPTER 12

EVE AND SYLVIE
France, 1943

The order of gloves she'd been working on was almost finished. Eve took a folded piece of paper out of her bag and opened it up. She never felt she had a talent for drawing things from memory; portraits had never been her forte either. Yet she thought she'd done a pretty good job of re-creating Luc's face on paper, seizing it from the swirling images that accompanied her constantly since their meeting. It was the next best thing to a photograph that she had of him. She looked up to see Bertrand standing alongside her and quickly put the drawing back in her bag. For once, Bertrand's eyes had a shine to them, as if he had something wonderful to tell her.

"I have an unusual order for you to work on when you've finished this one. Monsieur Lacroix, from rue de la Rose, wants us to make some women's gloves," he said. "Do you think you could design something special?"

"Well, that would be better than making these ugly gloves

for a change. *Maman* says I have a talent for design, but I've never been able to make anything special because of the war. I love that shop. Sylvie and I discovered it when we were doing some exploring the other day, but I thought Monsieur Lacroix sells shoes, not gloves."

"You've been good about going out and blending in, but I do worry about you," Bertrand said. "Did you hear that more Jewish families were rounded up yesterday? There are patrols everywhere."

"I heard people were put on trains. Is it true they are being taken to work camps? Why are they persecuting Jewish people like this? Who will be next?" Eve shook her head, her face creased with disbelief. "I wish we could do more to help them," she said.

"We are doing what we can. Several families have been guided to Spain by our operatives, but we can't save everyone."

Eve sighed and nodded her head sadly. "So, tell me, what does Monsieur Lacroix want us to make? Surely he can't have much demand for fancy gloves these days."

"A German officer wants matching shoes and gloves for his girlfriend. He's already chosen the shoes."

Eve pulled a face. She was about to say something, but Bertrand stopped her. He put up his hand.

"I know, I know. But there are some things we must do for the greater good. There is more to Monsieur Lacroix than meets the eye. This job will give you the perfect cover to collect messages from the old man on a regular basis."

"He's in our network?"

"Yes. If you see a pair of red shoes in the window, just say these words: 'We have a new supply of goatskin.' He'll answer: 'That's just what I need.'"

Rue de la Rose was a meandering street that led off Place de la Grenette. Eve imagined that the street must have been just as busy as Friars Lane in Worcester was before the war, but now, with soldiers wandering up and down, even the most fearless residents were too frightened to window shop. Turning into the street, she kept her head down and ignored the man who was idling beside a lamppost with a cigarette in one hand and his gun casually in the other. Monsieur Lacroix's shoe shop sat between a bookshop and a couturier. A pair of peep-toed pink satin shoes caught her eye. She stared longingly at them, for a moment quite forgetting the reason for her visit. Then she noticed the red pair. She opened the door and a sharp but not unpleasant smell of leather and shoe polish drifted towards her.

"*Bonjour, Mademoiselle.*"

An elderly man poked his head out from behind a door at the back of the shop. He held a hammer in his hand. "*Je peux vous aider?*"

"*Bonjour, Monsieur.* I've come from *La Ganterie Dupuis*. We have a new supply of goatskin."

"*Enchanté, Mademoiselle.*" Monsieur Lacroix put down the hammer. He limped towards her: one leg was shorter than the other and his longer leg dragged on the floor. "That's just what I need— I would like you to design something special for me. It is for a particularly important member of the Gestapo, and he expects the finest quality."

"I'm sure we will be able to come up with something unique for him."

He pulled out four boxes of shoes from the shelf behind the counter and opened them up. "These are the shoes he has bought. You'll find what you need in this one," he said, patting his hand on the box atop the pile.

As she was looking inside the boxes, the door opened. The German soldier she had seen on the corner walked in. She looked up at Monsieur Lacroix.

"May I look at those gorgeous pink shoes in the window while I am here? What size are they?"

"We will see, Mademoiselle. The perfect shoe for a pretty girl." Monsieur Lacroix shuffled over to the window, bringing attention to his wooden leg. He wobbled slightly as he reached the display in the window, knocking over a stack of shoe boxes. As the soldier rushed to his side to help him, Eve quickly took the note out of the shoe box Monsieur Lacroix had pointed out to her. She slipped the piece of paper into her pocket.

"They are a size thirty-eight," Monsieur Lacroix shouted across to her as he limped back with the shoes in his hand.

"That's a shame. They're far too big, but I could probably never afford them anyway." Eve said with exaggerated sadness. She looked at her watch. "I'm sorry, Monsieur, but I have to get back to work. I hadn't realized how late it is. I'll come back another day. I have an idea for the glove design now that I've seen the shoes. I won't need to take the boxes with me. I'll be back in the next couple of days. *Au revoir.*" She felt for the message in her pocket. It wasn't there.

"Mademoiselle," the soldier said. He followed her to the door. "You've dropped something." He bent down and picked up the crumpled missive from the floor.

"How stupid of me. My design notes," she said, taking it from him. "I wouldn't have got far without them. Thank you." Her heart was in her throat, but she somehow managed to give him her special smile.

Design was Eve's passion, and she was thrilled to be able to put her skills to work, but Bertrand had other plans for her before she could make a start on the project.

"It's the two British airmen hiding in Madame Valois' *boulangerie*," he said. "An airlift has been arranged to take them to England. I need you to go with Jules and be his interpreter. The men speak no French."

They were sitting outside at the *bar-tabac* where Bertrand was sipping a glass of red wine, while Eve ate a meager lunch of a hard-boiled egg with a small piece of *baguette.*

"I'm not too worried about the route you have to take. There aren't any checkpoints between the village and the airstrip right now. There's a pick-up scheduled for them tonight."

At half-past six that evening, Eve met Jules and Bertrand's contact, a man called Benoit. She'd cycled over to a churchyard on the edge of town where Benoit was waiting in the driver's seat of a Citroen *camionette,* with Jules already seated alongside him. Eve squeezed herself in next to Jules. He gave her a quick grin.

"Are you ready?"

"As ready as I'll ever be." She slammed the door shut, balancing her bag on her knees.

Benoit turned the key in the ignition, urging the truck to sputter to life. It shuddered reluctantly. They sat shoulder to shoulder, crammed tightly in the cab of the Citroen. Each time the wheels went through a pothole, the threesome all moved in unison, as if they were glued together. It was Jules who broke their nervous silence.

"Jolly good show, old chaps..." Eve realized he was speaking with a thick Spanish accent. He laughed and continued in French "They're the only words of English I know. I hope you know more, otherwise those poor men are going to be in trouble. Luckily my French is much better."

"Well, lucky for us, I don't speak it as badly as you. We'd all be in a right pickle if I did," Eve said. "Where do you come from, Jules?"

"Barcelona. My parents died just before I turned fifteen, and I've been looking after myself ever since. They were killed fighting Franco's forces."

"How did you end up in France?"

"I came with a group of refugees and joined the Resistance." He put his finger to his mouth and chewed nervously. She looked at his hands and noticed that all his nails were bitten to the quick.

By the time they reached their destination, Eve had learned that Jules had left a sister in Spain. He didn't get along with his uncle and aunt who had been taking care of them. He'd travelled from Spain to France with little money and by using his wits. She admired his fearlessness, and although he was much younger than she, she thought he was probably a lot more street smart, even if he was a bit of a chatterbox. He was funny, doing impersonations that had them in fits of laughter. He told them of his ambitions of someday becoming an actor and that when the War was over, he planned to go to Hollywood to follow his dreams.

It was dark by the time Benoit drove the truck into the village. A pale moon lit the square, and shadows lay ghostlike on the cobblestones. He pulled up outside the *boulangerie* and turned off the engine. Eve wound down the truck's window. Across the square, three men sat drinking at a table outside the bar, the tips of their cigarettes glowing in the dim light. Something small and black swooped in the inky black sky above the truck. Then several more flew down, narrowly missing each other. Eve's heart tightened in her chest as she realized they were bats; she'd never liked the spooky creatures.

"Is this it—are we there?" she asked.

"Yes," Jules said. "You'll have to come with me to explain to the men that they are being flown out tonight. It's important you tell them to keep quiet."

Just as they were about to get out of their truck, they heard the rattle of an engine slowing down as another truck pulled into the square from the opposite direction. It stopped outside the bar. Four German soldiers got out and went inside. The light flashing out of the open door now revealed that the men seated outside were staring across at them. They seemed to be agitated about something. One was gesticulating furiously. Then he banged his fist on the table.

"*Merde!* The timing couldn't be worse. Come on, we have to get a move on." Jules got out of the truck. He knocked on the door of the *boulangerie*. After a couple of minutes, a light went on in the shop and Madame Valois opened the door.

"Go around to the back," she hissed. "We're being watch-ed."

She gave a slight nod of her head to indicate that the men across the street were looking their way. Then she shouted for everyone to hear, "Deliveries are around the back!" She slammed the door in their faces.

"What are we going to do?" Eve gripped Jules' arm.

"Okay," he said. "Here's the plan. You two take the truck, pick up the airmen, and get away as quickly as you can. I'm going to cause a commotion to distract them in the bar."

"How?" she said.

"I don't know. I'll think of something—but you have to get going if you are to get the men to the pick-up on time."

"You're crazy. How will you get back to Grenoble?" Eve asked.

"Get going and stop asking questions."

"Okay. I'll take care of things here. Don't worry," she said. "But promise me you won't do anything silly." She touched him on the shoulder. He gave her a lopsided grin that made him look even younger than his fifteen years. Putting his hands in his pockets, he sauntered breezily across the square to the bar, as if he was going to meet his mates for a drink. Benoit was back in the truck already, revving the engine. She got into the passenger seat. The Frenchman maneuvered the vehicle down the narrow back alley behind the bakery. Madame Valois had by now opened the back door and was waiting for them. The two airmen were standing behind her in the dimly lit doorway. One was wearing a jacket and a pair of trousers that were far too small for him, the other an overcoat over his RAF uniform, his arm hanging in a sling. As they approached, Eve spoke quietly to them in English. "Hello there," she said. "We're going to get you home. We'll drive you to an airstrip about ten miles away. If all goes well, you'll be picked up by a British Lysander tonight and flown back to England." She opened the back door of the van, indicating where she wanted the men to hide.

"Thanks awfully for your help." The taller of the two men spoke in a plummy English accent. He picked an old sack that was lying in the back of the truck and tossed it to one side.

"Shush—don't talk," she growled. "There are Nazi soldiers only a few yards away. I'm sorry, but I'll have to cover you with those sacks. They don't smell too good."

The injured airman was shivering violently, barely able to support himself.

"We weren't told that one of you was sick. If we're stopped, you're going to have to keep him as still as possible," she snapped. "We'll all be shot if they find you."

A sour smell hit her as she opened the van door. She sat in the passenger seat wrinkling her nose. Benoit wiped the sweat off his face with a dirty rag, his head swiveling from side to side anxiously. Across the square, a crowd had gathered outside the bar. It looked like a fight had just started between Jules and another man. Eve put her hand to her mouth and gripped Benoit, her nails digging into his arm. "Get going before they see us!" she said urgently.

Benoit glanced over his shoulder. His clammy hand slipped off the gear stick as he crunched into third gear. They sped off out of the village.

"*Merde*! Don't look back," he said. "Jules is in trouble."

The following morning, Eve was waiting outside her uncle's office door when Celeste interrupted her.

"What do you want him for? Perhaps I can help you."

"I have a question about the gloves I am making for Monsieur Lacroix. When will it be convenient to speak to him?" Eve asked.

"You're quite the busy little bee, aren't you? Making yourself so useful. I don't know how we managed before you arrived."

Eve ignored the sneering in Celeste's voice, not wanting to rise to the woman's bait.

"Go in—I'm sure he'll see you. Little Eve seems to be his favorite these days."

Eve knocked again on the office door, before opening it. Her uncle looked up expectantly.

"Oh yes, Eve—have you finished the designs?" he asked. He lowered his voice.

"What happened last night?" he whispered.

"It was a close one. I don't know how we got out of there unnoticed. It was swarming with soldiers. As we left, another carload of them arrived. It was intense. But Jules saved the day. That boy will make quite an actor one day. He was fearless—he threw himself into the middle of it all to distract them. Goodness knows what he did or said to them. Have you heard what happened to him?"

"We don't know for sure, but the contact I have with the police has said someone matching his description has been taken to Gestapo headquarters. But he couldn't confirm it. They have Madame Valois in custody though. I'm not sure what happened. We need to find out who informed on her. The poor woman," Bertrand said.

He took off his glasses and rubbed his eyes. Eve noticed the dark circles under his eyes looked more pronounced than ever.

"I'm concerned that you will be exposed if she or Jules

talks," he said.

"One of her neighbors must have ratted on her. I don't think she saw me for long enough to know who I am. But if they have Jules, how will he survive? He's full of bravado, but I can't help but feel that he is a bit overconfident. He's only a boy and a big chatterbox."

"I know, *chérie*. He does have a lot of swagger, and I worry, too, what he will do under duress. I'm afraid for you all; you're out in the thick of it." He put his arms around her and kissed the top of her head. "But you're all just kids—you must be careful. I can't believe I brought you here. Your *maman* would be angry if she knew. No one must know who you are. I suggest you lie low. I want you and Sylvie to stick to transmitting and nothing else for a while. The gloves for Monsieur Lacroix should keep you busy."

When Eve returned to Madame Corot's house the following week to pick up the gloves, she found Luc sitting on the wall next to the church. A bubble of joy burst in her stomach, sending butterflies fluttering through her body.

"You came!" she said breathlessly.

Jumping up, he smiled back at her, brushing his long blonde hair out of his eyes.

"Of course. I've been waiting a while. I didn't know what time you'd be coming. How's your leg?"

"Much better thank you. You did a great job of cleaning it up. Madame Corot told me you're training to be a doctor."

"Yes, I am. Would you like to go for a walk when you've finished your business with her?" he asked.

"I'd love to," Eve replied. She gripped the handlebars of her bicycle as she started to feel dizzy. Her heart was beating fast. Taking a deep breath she said, "Perhaps you could walk part of the way home with me. I wouldn't expect you to come all the way back to the city, but if you've time, I'd love the company..." Once she'd started to talk, she couldn't stop her nervous chatter. "It's a lovely walk, the trees, mountains. There's nowhere like this where I come from, perhaps you can show me around."

Luc grinned at her.

"I'm so glad you're happy to see me. Hurry up and collect your gloves. I've brought a picnic with me. We can stop for lunch by the river, and you can tell me all about yourself."

Later they sat by the water and Luc unwrapped some slices of ham which he handed to Eve with a piece of bread. She took a bite of ham, suddenly feeling shy and tongue-tied.

"How long have you been a glovemaker for?" Luc asked breaking the silence.

Eve took a deep breath realizing she couldn't tell him the truth and it was going to be difficult to lie to him.

"I've always been around gloves," she said slowly, improvising as she went on. "My parents had a glove factory in Paris. But everything fell apart when *les Allemandes* invaded. They sent my father to Germany to work and then *Maman* got sick. She died."

Luc reached out and touched her hand.

"I'm sorry," he said. "My mother is dead too."

Eve looked down at her hands, unable to look him in the eye.

"I'd rather not talk about it. Tell me more about you," she said.

Luc didn't let go of her hand and when she finally looked up, the compassion in his eyes melted her heart. It was so wrong to deceive him, but she had no choice.

"I'm taking a medical degree at the University of Grenoble. I want to be a family doctor and give back to the people in my community. When my mother was ill, everyone rallied around to help us," Luc said. "I owe them so much."

'I just make gloves," Eve replied. "I'm not helping anyone."

"Yes, you are," Luc said. "You're helping people keep warm!"

Eve giggled. "I suppose I am, but you're special." She reached up and touched his face with her hand. "I've never met anyone like you," she said.

"And I've never met anyone who makes me feel the way you do." He leaned into her and stole a kiss.

Eve felt her face turn pink.

"I hope we can spend some more time together," she said shyly.

"I'm busy helping my papa on the farm right now, but when the weather gets colder, there won't be so much to do. Do you ski?"

"No, I've never been skiing. There's not much snow where I come from."

"Well, in that case, it would be my pleasure to teach you."

"I'd love that. But I have to tell you, I'm not at all athletic. Coming up that mountain road the other day on my bike almost killed me!"

Luc reached for her hand.

"Let's hope *les Boches* don't come looking for me and send me to Germany. Now that I've found you, I don't want to lose you. Would you mind if I kissed you again?"

"I thought you'd never ask," Eve said, suddenly feeling quite bold.

She shuddered slightly as Luc put his arms around her. When his lips touched hers, she made a wish. She wished that one day he would ask her to marry him. She knew she had found the man of her dreams.

Eve had been waiting for the right time to tell Sylvie about Luc after her second meeting with him. She'd been dying to share her news with her friend, but they'd just been too busy. It came as a surprise to her, though, when Sylvie challenged her one evening.

"What's the matter with you, Eve? You've got a secret smile on your face all the time," Sylvie said. "Has something happened that you haven't told me about?"

"I've been meaning to tell you—I can't stop thinking about him."

"Who? Is it that medical student who fixed your leg for you last week? How do you know he's reliable? He could be a spy. We can't risk jeopardizing our mission."

"Yes, that's him. It's not like I planned it or anything. I don't think you need to worry about him, though. I can't describe it, but it was like there was this electric current running between us, and I couldn't let go, *and* he has the most amazing blue eyes you have ever seen! He's gorgeous." She shivered. "I saw him again yesterday. He's the one, I know he is."

"I can understand that feeling when you've fallen for someone—will you promise to keep this a secret?"

"Of course, secrets and lies are our job."

"No, this is a secret about me." Sylvie blushed slightly and looked down at her shoes. "I'm in love with Marie and she feels the same way about me. I never really understood how I felt about women until I met her. Then it all made sense. You don't think badly of me, do you?"

Eve grasped Sylvie's hand. "Oh, Sylvie. Why would I think badly of you? I don't care who you love. You're my best friend and the sister I always wanted. But you've got to be so careful. I've heard what *les Allemandes* do to homosexuals—I don't want to think about what they might do to you, if they find out you're a lesbian."

"I know. But I can't deny how I feel."

"I'm so proud of you for telling me. You're not frightened to be yourself. That's why I love you."

Despite the concerns that their network might be exposed, Eve and Sylvie continued to transmit and receive messages as Bertrand suggested. They made radio contact with England at night, and during the day they continued their work in the glove factory.

Monsieur Duron's *bar-tabac* was now the Gestapo's favorite place to drink. While it was risky having German soldiers drinking just yards away from them, in some ways it was safe to be so close and see what was going on outside. On the nights when they weren't transmitting or receiving messages, they would switch on the BBC's broadcast to France. Keeping the volume turned down low, they listened to coded phrases which would sometimes indicate the timing of the next parachute drop of arms or supplies. When they heard the words *"le chamois bondit,"* they knew it was directed to them.

"Got it," Eve whispered. She quickly started to write down the English words that followed: *"Emile needs a haircut. I can do it for him on Tuesday. Tell him he should come to the same place."* Sylvie took out their decoding book. She quickly deciphered what the message relayed.

"We need to get this message to your uncle as soon as possible. London is planning a weapons-drop tomorrow."

As she spoke, the sound of a car door closing outside in the square made her look up. A German military car had pulled up in the road alongside the bar. The whining and crackling noise of the radio seemed to fill the room, mingling with their own nervous energy.

"Quick! Hide everything. There's a car that's pulled up outside. It could be using a radio detector," Sylvie whispered loudly.

Eve placed the radio together with the transmitter and the crystals needed for transmission in the small suitcase, nestling them next to the receiver. She pried open a floorboard under the bed, pushing everything into the space. She placed her decoding books under the mattress.

The driver of the Mercedes staff car got out and opened the rear passenger door. He clicked his heels together and saluted as Gruppenführer Müller stepped out. He sat down at one of the tables nearest to the curb, and snapped his fingers in the air, summoning Monsieur Duron to bring him his usual wine. Earlier, before the barkeeper had been able to hide his wine stock, Müller had confiscated it, setting aside the better wines for his own consumption. A faint light from the bar filtered out onto the sidewalk, and the man sat nursing his drink. As he lit a cigarette, they could smell the fumes wafting in through their bedroom window.

"It's just that disgusting man again." Sylvie turned away from the window and shivered, "I can't bear to look at him—he makes me feel sick."

"Do you think it's safe to get back to what we were doing?" Eve pulled her decoding books out from under the mattress. "I want to double-check that I wrote everything down correctly."

"Yes—I can hear them singing now," Sylvie replied. "They're making quite a racket—they're all as happy as larks. I'll close the window."

As the weather turned colder and the days shorter, Monsieur Duron took the tables and chairs inside the bar. The soldiers still came and went, but it was a relief to no longer see them hanging around outside in the street all night. Eve and Sylvie continued with their transmissions, with one of them always on the lookout.

The network started to grow under Eve's management. People were eager to help. The population of Grenoble and people in the surrounding countryside were becoming increasingly frustrated by the Vichy government's collusion with *les Allemandes*. Hunger became more widespread as their precious food supplies were diverted to feed the German army. Eve managed to enlist several schoolteachers, who were able to travel without question from village to village. They didn't take much convincing that they needed to contribute in some way. A chain of contacts was formed to pass on key messages and help conceal Jewish families and Allied soldiers trying to get back to the safety of England. Many of these brave people were women whose husbands, brothers, or sons had left home to fight with the Resistance. But life for the inexperienced *maquisards* hiding out in the mountains was grueling and receiving support from the network was crucial. Some were lucky enough to be living in derelict *chalets* or farmhouses, but others were living in wretched conditions in the limestone caves of the Vercors massif, dressed in the same summer clothes that they had left home in months earlier. Drops of supplies became less frequent as the winter took hold. The only food that the *maquis* now ate was either stolen or supplied by women like Madame Corot, who left baskets of *pâté,* cheese, and bread in hiding places in the woods.

"*Bonjour,* Monsieur," Eve said as she entered Monsieur Lacroix's shoe shop. The pair of red shoes was prominently displayed in the window.

"Mademoiselle Eve, I've some important news," the old man said. His eyes darted to the shop door before he stepped close to her and whispered, "I've heard that the latest airdrop of explosives has fallen into the wrong hands. A Communist group have bombed a German munitions train. Eleven of our fighters have been killed in retaliation. We needed that route to gain access to other targeted infrastructure. That plan is no longer possible. You must tell Bertrand we have to come up with another one—and to expect more reprisals."

"This is exactly what we feared. What a mess." She kissed him on both cheeks. "I'll tell him immediately."

In late November, Bertrand asked Eve and Sylvie to liaise with a group of men in the mountains who had a cache of Sten guns that needed to be repaired. Another young partisan named Robert, whom Bertrand had recommended for his dependability, escorted them. He was only nineteen years old, and he, like Jules, was already well-known with the *maquis* for his courage. They went to a schoolhouse in a village in the mountains. A class was in session. Through an open window, they could hear the children reciting their multiplication tables in their sing-song voices.

"*Trois fois cinq, quinze; quatre fois cinq, vingt...*"

A side door led to the basement. Opening it, they were hit by a wall of cigarette smoke and desperation. Three men were sitting around a table examining a gun.

The self-appointed leader of the group stood up, his body taut and defensive. He looked like he was having a terrible day. He rubbed his nicotine-stained fingers over his stubbly chin and spat on the floor. Then his bloodshot eyes wandered over to the girls, as if his day had just got even worse.

"What are they doing here? I thought you were bringing someone to fix the guns—when's the mechanic coming?"

"Sylvie is the mechanic," Robert said. "And Eve has come to help her. They're good at what they do. You're lucky to have them here."

Used to her skills being so readily dismissed, Sylvie didn't even bother to acknowledge the man. She pushed past him over to where the guns were stacked. "Let me take a look," she said. She picked up a weapon and quickly evaluated the damage.

Eve took the gun out of Sylvie's hand.

"What do you think is wrong with them?" she asked her friend.

"The firing mechanism is broken." Sylvie turned to look at the leader of the group.

"Are they all like this?"

"Some of them are. They came in an airdrop a week ago. Others have the stock broken. We don't have the manuals to help us fix them, otherwise we would have mended them ourselves. How are you going to be able to help us?"

Eve shrugged off her coat and thick gloves.

"Sylvie has been trained to mend most weapons that the Allies are sending. Be careful when you use these Sten guns though. Unfortunately, the weapons they're providing are cheap and inferior. We've heard that they jam easily and if you drop one it'll unload the entire magazine. I've already sent a message to headquarters to request better equipment."

"Yes, some aren't at all well designed," Sylvie said. "I'll do my best to fix the broken for you."

The man's eyes widened in surprise. "I'm impressed—thanks for the advice. I didn't know women knew anything about guns. I thought the problem was that my men didn't know how to use these weapons and had broken them. My name's Antoine. I'm happy to have you here." He slapped Sylvie on the back and grinned at Eve.

"It's not your men's fault—just be careful how you use them in future," Eve said.

Sylvie inspected the gun. She took no time stripping it down, tweaking the mechanism, and putting it back together correctly. The men watched, awed by her skill and precision. As each weapon was fixed, Eve oiled and reassembled it as Sylvie had shown her.

They'd been working for about an hour when they heard a truck pulling up outside and then doors slamming. Antoine put his finger to his lips, indicating that they were all to keep quiet. The sound of heavy footsteps thumped on the ceiling above their heads. The children stopped singing.

"You have to get out of here now—it sounds like trouble," Antoine whispered. He pointed to a trap door in the floor. He grabbed the girls' coats and hats and pushed them through the opening. "There's a passageway that leads to a copse on the outskirts of the village. Keep moving and don't stop until you find somewhere to hide in the woods. I am concerned about what will happen if our cache is discovered—we'll have to stay here."

Eve and Sylvie started down the dark passageway. Above their heads, they could hear someone playing the piano and the children starting to sing again. Robert was following close behind. "*Mademoiselle* Segal is a brave woman," he said. "I pray she's able to convince the soldiers that she has nothing to hide."

At the end of the passageway, there was a flimsy trapdoor that was latched from the inside. Robert pushed on a rusty bolt and slowly opened the flap. Climbing up the rough-hewn steps into an opening above ground, they saw a thicket of trees. They could hear the clack-clack of gunshots coming from behind them.

"We have to help," Sylvie said urgently, turning back towards the steps. "Those poor children must be terrified."

"We can't Sylv. We have to get back to let Bertrand know what's happened. There's nothing we can do," Eve said.

Robert grabbed Sylvie roughly by the arm. "My grandfather used to hunt in these woods. Sometimes I went with him. I think I can get us back to Grenoble without being seen. Keep low to the ground and try not to make any noise with your feet—hurry up."

As they ran, another volley of gunshots crackled in the air. Sylvie turned to look behind again, but Robert pulled her hand.

"I can't leave them—I'm going back!" she said. Eve watched in dismay as Sylvie broke away from Robert and ran back towards the school.

As Sylvie reached a clearing in the woods, Eve started after her, but Robert held her tight.

"I'm not going to let you die too," he growled.

Looking towards the schoolyard, Eve could see Mademoiselle Segal and the children lined up against the wall of the building. Three Nazi soldiers stood in front of them, their guns drawn. The senior officer walked slowly towards her. He grabbed the teacher by her hair. "This is what you get for not talking! Bitch!" he shouted. He lifted the barrel of his rifle and brought it down on the teacher's head. The woman fell to the ground. A piercing scream rang out as one little girl ran to *Mademoiselle* Segal's side and threw herself on the woman's body.

"The children!" she whispered. The thought that she was about to witness children being slaughtered was overwhelming and her head was swimming.

She closed her eyes and opened them again, willing that what she had just witnessed would disappear. She struggled to breathe, her heart pounding in her chest. Then something triggered in her brain; the drills she had been taught in Scotland flashed in front of her eyes. With a rush of adrenalin fueling her courage, she crept on her elbows and knees, staying low to the ground, her handgun at the ready. Robert by this time was at her side.

"You're crazy. You're going to get us all killed!" he snapped.

She put her finger to her lips to silence him, and together they crawled towards the schoolyard where they hid next to Sylvie behind a low stone wall. Eve locked eyes with Sylvie and Robert. She nodded towards the soldier she was going to shoot, indicating to them the ones they were to take down. But before she could fire her weapon, she saw Sylvie fall to the

148

ground, hit by a bullet from a hidden sniper. Blood oozed from her friend's jacket and her eyes opened wide in surprise. Sylvie slumped forward grasping her heart, her head hitting the wall.

As Robert worked fast, firing at the three soldiers, killing them one after the other, Eve crawled over to where Sylvie lay. She reached her friend and watched in horror as blood continued to flow onto the ground from the wound in her chest. She felt for a pulse in her neck. Sylvie was dead. A silent shriek stuck in Eve's throat, and she thought her heart might stop beating.

After the rapid gunfire, the schoolyard was eerily silent. The children stood petrified like stone statues and in the woods the birds had stopped singing. Eve was still finding it hard to breathe. She watched as Robert looked frantically around him, searching for the remaining soldier. Between the stone wall where they were hiding and the schoolhouse stood a large oak tree. Another shot rang out. The sound triggered the anger inside her. She estimated that if she could get behind the tree, she would be able to get a good shot at the sniper. She darted forward with a burst of anger-fueled energy and hit the trunk of the tree with force. A bullet hit the bark above her head and ricocheted off. The soldier started to move from behind a metal dustbin. With Robert now beside her, Eve took aim and they both fired at the man. The dustbin rattled loudly as the German fell on top of it and it rolled slowly into the school-yard. A piercing wail cut through the silence. It took several seconds for Eve to realize it was coming from her own mouth.

The pair made their way back to the city, taking seldom-used animal tracks down the mountainside, through the thickly wooded and snowy terrain. Each step Eve took felt heavier than the last, weighed down by what she had seen and done. They had left hastily, unwelcome intruders in a village that had no idea the Resistance was working among them. She had been forced to abandon Sylvie where she had fallen, with no idea of what would become of her friend's body. The sun had long set by the time he reached Grenoble and the glove factory, where Bertrand was waiting for the girls to return. Eve pushed open the door to Bertrand's office. She didn't speak; still covered in Sylvie's blood, she collapsed into his arms. Her uncle grabbed her as her knees gave way, holding her tightly in his arms and rocking her back and forth as she sobbed.

In the days after Sylvie's death, Eve couldn't even mourn her friend properly. Not only were they unable to find out what had become of her body, but they had to hide the fact that she was no longer alive. She and Bertrand concocted a story that Sylvie had returned to Paris for a family emergency. Then reprisals came quickly, and more people from the village were killed in retaliation for the death of the German soldiers. The Gestapo took *Mademoiselle* Segal for questioning. She only survived for a couple of days, succumbing to the injuries she had sustained during the raid. The only blessing in the whole wretched episode was that they had saved the lives of fifteen children. Eve thought that it would have been easier if she had become a soldier. Subversive life in the Resistance was far more complicated.

CHAPTER 13

EVE
France, 1943

E ve trudged her way to work through pillows of newly fallen snow, the white rooftops of the buildings glistening in the morning sun. The scene reminded her of a snow globe her parents had given her when she was a child, but this thought did nothing to dispel her grief. She never knew it was possible to miss someone so much and wondered if the pain would ever go away.

"*Bonjour,* Monsieur," she said to her uncle as she entered the factory floor.

Celeste was hovering nearby. She put her hands on her hips and gave Eve one of her challenging looks. "You must be missing your little friend; have you heard from her yet? I imagine it must have been difficult for her to return to Paris with all the fighting going on."

"No, I haven't heard from her," Eve replied. "I hope her mother is still alive when she gets there." She looked down at her shoes and bit the inside of her cheek to stop herself from crying.

Bernard touched her arm gently.

"Eve, *les Boches* are picking up that big order this morning. Can you and Marie box it up, please? Then I need you to work in the dye room."

Eve trembled slightly and nodded. "Of course, Monsieur."

Marie was busy cutting leather and looked up when she heard her name mentioned. She put down her scissors. "Any news from Sylvie yet? I don't understand why she left without telling me where she was going."

"I know. It all happened very quickly," Eve said. "I hope we hear from her soon." She was unable to look Marie in the eye. Lying had become second nature now, but it felt wrong that she couldn't tell Marie the truth. She knew how Marie felt about Sylvie. She of all people deserved to know that her girlfriend was dead. "Come on, let's get these gloves packed up," was all she was able to say.

When the boxes were stacked and ready to be picked up, Eve went about her next task. She followed the strict rules for working in the confined space. Once inside, she locked the door behind her. She took a mask off a hook on the wall, put it over her mouth, and set about mixing a black dye. It took several minutes before she achieved the exact color *les Allemandes* required for their flight gloves. If the gloves didn't meet their expectations, as had happened in the past, they would simply destroy the order and demand more be made. The factory couldn't afford any losses.

As she carefully applied the dark stain to lengths of animal skin, she let her mind wander to Luc. She had to see him again. She knew she couldn't tell him about Sylvie or about her work with the Resistance, but she desperately needed his comfort; he was the only person who made her feel safe.

She'd been working for about twenty minutes when she heard several vehicles screech to a halt in the road outside. At first, she thought that it must be the Germans coming to pick up their order of gloves and was about to go out to help. But something made her hesitate. She listened as doors creaked open, followed by the clatter of heavy hobnailed boots and angry voices. Terror rose in her throat as gunshots rang in her ears, and she heard a bullet ricochet off the metal door that she was standing behind. She looked around the small space for somewhere to hide. Her only hope was that les Boches would not be able to open the heavy security door, and she quietly checked the key in the lock and ran the bolt to reassure herself that it was secure. Reaching for the light switch, she turned off the overhead light bulb and curled in a ball behind a large barrel.

As she lay trembling in her hiding place, the sounds on the other side of the door were terrifying. She heard the screams of her friends as they were dragged out of the building by snarling soldiers. Time seemed to stand still, but the raid only took minutes before she heard Celeste's tremulous voice say that there was no one else in the building. Then the growling, guttural voices faded away, taken over by the sound of revving engines that told her that they were leaving. The situation was worse than she could have ever imagined. Until Sylvie's death, while she hadn't exactly felt invincible, she'd always believed that they were on the winning team. She'd put faith in her Uncle Bertrand that no one would consider the glove factory to be a Resistance operation. He'd done everything in his power to keep it a secret, but someone must have talked. Her mind whirled at the implications that she hadn't before considered. It had been a bad idea for Bertrand to send her with Sylvie to mend the weapons. Her job as a courier was now in jeopardy and she would no longer be able to deliver messages unnoticed. Someone had recognized her and Sylvie and had connected them to the factory. The Gestapo were ruthless, and they would stop at nothing until they found everyone involved.

Still too petrified to move, she cowered down behind vats. She thought she might faint, overcome by fumes and fear of what had happened on the other side of the door. She was terrified of what she would see when she opened it. She waited for hours in the dark, windowless room until she heard nothing but silence. While she waited, she prayed that her uncle would be able to convince the Gestapo that he was innocent of any involvement with the partisans. Now she would have to disappear if she was to be of any help. The network was in danger, and she had work to do. She prayed that the Germans knew nothing of her existence.

A strong smell of cordite hit her as she eased the dye room door open. The hinges squeaked, echoing eerily in the empty space. The factory floor was in ruins, bolts of leather slashed to pieces, sewing machines smashed and tables and chairs strewn everywhere. Eve crept slowly through the debris, looking cautiously around her for any sign of life. But everyone was gone. She was alone.

It was dark outside, but she was able to see, guided by the brightness of the snow cover. However, everything looked different, as she made her way to the mountain road that led to Madame Corot's house. She wasn't sure she was going the right way and it was only when she saw the road drop away to the valley that she felt a surge of relief. It was close to where Luc had told her he lived with his father. Her need to see him was overwhelming. She changed her plan. If she took the track off the main route, perhaps she could find his house. He would help her get a message to Madame Corot; she knew he would.

She had been walking for about half an hour when wood smoke tickled her nose and, looking into the distance, she saw the outline of a farmhouse etched on the night sky. Her heart pumped impatiently in her chest as she set off running towards it, slipping, and sliding, her eyes fixed on her goal ahead.

The snow had fallen in deep drifts on the track, but she kept on pressing forward in her eagerness to reach the house and Luc. Turning a sharp bend in the road, she didn't notice a metal plough that was hidden by the snowfall. Her foot caught the hard edge of the machine and slipping on the icy surface of the road, she hit the ground heavily. She heard a crack as her leg twisted awkwardly under her, then everything went black.

It was daybreak as Luc skied his way down the mountain. The early morning sun was forcing its way up through the streaky gray sky, leaving rose-striated patterns on the snowy surface. The branches of the pine trees on either side of the run dipped under the weight of the newly fallen snow. He was an excellent skier and expertly propelled his way through the fresh powder, his leg muscles working to flex and extend his skis downwards, popping in and out of deep drifts. With the whoosh of icy snowflakes brushing his face, he powered through the ocean of glistening snow

By this time, he had joined up with a group of *maquisards*. The Germans extended the work ruling to all young men regardless of their educational status, but Luc was able to escape into the mountains the day the *Milice* came looking for him. His family had a lucky break too. His father knew one of the policemen from when he was a child and used to go fishing with him. It was because of this connection that Monsieur Gaspard avoided being arrested, and his farm was left undamaged. Other families in the area were not so fortunate; the Vichy police were every bit as ruthless as the German military.

But even for Luc, hiding in the mountains was difficult. The group that he was now fighting with was disorganized and lacked direction. A farmworker took on the responsibility of training the men, but there was resentment to his leadership, and without guns or ammunition it seemed pointless anyway.

As he neared the farm he slowed down, turning his skis sideways and planting the poles, before coming to a stop in front of the barn. He removed his skis and, leaning them up against the wall, cautiously peered through the opening of the barn door. Inside, he saw his father and brother leaning over someone in the far corner of the drafty space.

"Thank goodness you're here, Luc."

"Who is she?" Luc knelt next to his father.

"I don't know but be careful—her leg is in bad shape."

Eve lay on the ground, covered with a blanket, her face turned to the wall. She didn't move.

Eve remained unconscious as they moved her into the farmhouse and made her as comfortable as possible. Her leg was broken. Luc did his best to set it with splints that his father roughly cut from some lumber in the farmyard. The uneven splints were not ideal but were all that was available to them; fortunately, she remained asleep throughout the procedure of manipulating the bone back into place. Her temperature was elevated, and Luc applied cold compresses continuously to cool her down and help break the fever. She slept for two days.

"Where am I?" Eve whispered hoarsely when she finally came to.

She was lying on a cot by the fireside. Luc was sitting on the edge of the bed, looking down at her.

She gave him a wobbly smile and sniffed weakly.

"Is it really you—and is that bacon I can smell?"

Luc touched her forehead. "Your temperature seems to have come down. Thank God you're alright. You've been out cold for two days or maybe more—I don't know how long you were in the barn before we found you. You were unconscious—you've broken your leg."

Her smile faded as a wave of pain hit her, the realization of what had happened tensing her body. She threw back the blanket and saw that her leg was splinted and tightly bandaged in what looked like tea towels.

"You seem to be making a habit of fixing my leg. How lucky can a girl be," she said with a grimace.

Then all the events of the previous days, the round-up, the screams of her friends, her flight to find help, came flooding back. She put her hand over her mouth in horror. "I need to let the network know what's happened..." She tried to get out of the bed. "You have to help me."

Luc gently pushed her down and handed her a glass of water.

"Drink this," he said. "What are you talking about?"

In uneven breaths, she started to tell him that she worked with the Resistance and that Madame Corot was one of her contacts.

"I thought you told me you made gloves. You're working with the partisans?"

"Yes, I am a glovemaker. That's my cover."

She was about to add that she was a British agent, but then thought better of it. She had signed an oath of secrecy to her country that could never be broken. All she could tell him was that she was working with the Resistance. She needed his help.

"The glove factory is the center of the network. Jules is a young Spanish kid working with the Resistance. He was arrested a few weeks ago when we were moving some British airmen. The Germans killed my friend Sylvie two weeks ago in Vassieux."

His eyes widened. "I would never have guessed it. And Madame Corot too. Why didn't you tell me any of this before? You know, you're not going to be able to do anything for quite some time. You won't be able to put any weight on your leg for weeks; after that, there'll be months of rehabilitation. I hope I've set it right. My orthopedic experience is non-existent."

Eve looked down at her injured leg in dismay. It throbbed painfully. The thought that she wouldn't be able to stand on it for such a long time was daunting. She had a job to do and now she was of no use to anyone.

"I'm sorry, I couldn't tell you. You're our only hope now. You'll have to go to Madame Corot's house—there's no time to waste. Too many people have already died. And you must find out what has happened to Monsieur Dupuis. Please, do it for me," she pleaded.

He gripped her hand reassuringly. "I'll go right away—don't worry, I'll do what I can. You must rest. I'm not sure if I'm impressed with what you've been doing or if I think you're crazy, but right now you need someone to look after you. Eve Charlot, you are one very surprising girl."

CHAPTER 14

GEORGINA, EVE AND ANGELA
England, 2016

Georgina reached for her phone and switched off the recording app.

"Oh Grandy. I'm so sorry. Sylvie seemed so special."

"She died on a Thursday. I've never liked Thursdays to this day," Eve said. Her eyes were glassy as she kept talking. "She was an extraordinary woman. I met her parents when I got back to England. But I couldn't tell them how she had died. No one was permitted to talk about the SOE. I told them more lies." She whimpered.

"Thank goodness you had Luc."

"Luc and I had something that only very few people find in life. But it was so fleeting."

They heard footsteps on the stairs, followed by a tap on Eve's bedroom door. It was Eileen. "Hello, you two. I just wanted to let you know I'm back. I know you want to get over to your friend's house for lunch, Georgina."

She looked at Georgina and then Eve. "I'm sorry, am I

disturbing you?"

"No, dear, not at all. You're a breath of fresh air, just what I need right now." Eve braced herself to smile. "Have you had a nice time with your family?"

Listening to her grandmother, Georgina suddenly understood the steeliness of her character, the shifting of gears the old woman had perfected when she needed to avoid confronting her past. She'd witnessed it several times over the weeks she'd spent with her. She realized that not only was it a coping mechanism, but it was the backbone of her disappearing generation, the courage to move forward in adversity, pretending that everything was all right when it wasn't. Her grandmother epitomized the expression "stiff upper lip" that she'd often heard about but, being half American and her mother's daughter, had never signed up for.

"I've brought some leftovers with me—my girls were trying their hand at baking last night and the result was a chicken pie and a chocolate cake. Not bad for a first attempt. I hope you don't mind being a guinea pig, Eve," Eileen said.

Eve beamed. "You spoil me. That all sounds quite delicious."

Georgina touched Eileen's arm. "Thanks, Eileen, you're a lifesaver. If it's alright with you, Grandy, I'll be off—I should be back by early evening."

She kissed Eve's forehead. "I love you. Get some rest," she said. Her grandmother's story was exhausting; she needed a breather too.

Parked in the driveway of Camilla and Matt's house was a smart, open-topped sports car that sat low to the ground. Georgina was about to ring the doorbell when Camilla opened the door.

"That's fancy. I thought you said that Paul worked for an

ancestry website—they must pay well," said Georgina, turning around to take another quick look at the bright red car.

"Oh, I didn't tell you—he founded the company. He's done well for himself since you last saw him. Come in, the kids are excited to see you."

The hallway was warm and heavy with the smell of deliciousness.

"Oh my God, I haven't had a real English Sunday lunch for such a long time. It smells divine!" Georgina said, giving Camilla a hug.

From where she was standing, she could see into the family room where Matt and his friend Paul were sitting by the fireplace. They were each nursing a glass of red wine and munching peanuts.

"You two look comfy," she said. "Drinks at noon—my kind of people."

Paul stood up. He was taller than she remembered. His blonde hair stuck up on one side as if he'd just got out of bed, making him look slightly vulnerable. "Not exactly my type," she thought, but there was something about his broad shoulders, the way he held himself, that was oddly appealing. He was wearing chinos and a wool sweater over a button-down shirt, which Georgina had noticed seemed to be the uniform of some British men. She went up to him and kissed him on both cheeks.

"Nice to meet you again. I remember you were Matt's best man. All the girls were after you."

Paul ran his hands through his hair, messing it up even more. "I doubt that very much! I remember you too. You gave a funny speech about Camilla."

"Did I?" she said. "I'd forgotten that. I'd had far too much to drink by then."

Matt stood up. "Can I get you something to drink now?" he asked.

"No thanks. I'm on the wagon. Perhaps some sparkling

water if you have any."

He raised his eyebrows in surprise. "I've never heard you refuse a drink, Georgie," he said.

"I've put on a bit too much weight," she replied, patting her midriff. "Time to cut back for a while."

She sat down on the sofa, fluttered her eyelashes, and patted the cushion, inviting Paul to sit down next to her.

"Camilla tells me you're the man I need."

Paul fled to the safety of the chair opposite. "How's New York?" he asked hoarsely. He nervously cleared his throat and took a deep gulp from his wine glass. Georgina got up and sat on the arm of his chair.

"Oh, New York is boring. I want to hear more about you," she said. "I'd quite forgotten how handsome you are. Perhaps we could grab a drink one evening—just the two of us." She touched him, slowly running a manicured finger down his arm. "I love your sweater, by the way. It's cashmere, isn't it? I love a man with good taste in clothes."

As Matt came back with a glass of Perrier for Georgina, she couldn't help noticing the anxious look on Paul's face.

"Do you think you might be able to help Georgie find any family in France? Her gran was a spy during the War. She fell in love with a French chap named Luc. There's little else to go on, but Georgie has the family name and the village where they used to live. Apparently, Luc, Eve's boyfriend, had a younger brother—maybe he's still alive," Matt said.

Paul looked at Matt gratefully. "Well, if the birth, baptism, and death records have been catalogued by the local church, it should all be possible to find out online. Otherwise, you may have to go to France to do some sleuthing yourself. There are also DNA tests available now, so can go into even more depth. You never know, some of your relatives may be registered on our website and you'll discover a whole slew of unknown family members." Paul became increasingly animated as he continued to describe how to go about the process; once he started talking, there was no stopping him. Even though she was eager to find out about her grandfather, Georgina felt her eyes glazing over as he explained the benefits of genetic testing and genotyping.

"How about taking me for a spin in that car of yours after lunch? I'd love to hear more, then we wouldn't have to bore everyone else. Just the two of us," she said.

Paul shuffled uncomfortably in his chair and gave Matt a pleading look.

"We promised we'd take the kids outside to play after lunch," Matt said, as if that had been the plan all along. "I don't mind hearing all about it at all now, I'm finding it fascinating."

"I'm sorry if I've been boring you. I do go on a bit when I'm talking about my job," Paul said.

"Oh no, it's not boring at all. I'm finding it interesting too. You know an awful lot about this stuff," Georgina replied.

She continued to smile sweetly, even though she was somewhat confused that he didn't respond to her charms like most men tended to.

Camilla had outdone herself and cooked a perfect meal—from the perfectly pink roast beef to the crispy roast potatoes and fluffy Yorkshire puddings. For the first time in her life, Georgina devoured everything on her plate. Later the two women loaded the dishwasher while Matt and Paul took the children into the garden to play.

"Don't think I didn't notice you trying to hit on Paul. Go easy. He's not so experienced with women," Camilla said. "You'll eat him up and spit him out."

"I don't know what's wrong with me. It must be my hormones! He's not really my type anyway. He sounds a bit like a mad scientist with all that talk of autosomes and chromosomes or whatever. He looks a bit like one too. Oh, by the way—I forgot to tell you my mum is arriving tomorrow."

"Finally!" Camilla snorted.

Georgina realized by now that her mother was using the cruise as an excuse not to visit her and her grandmother. Georgina questioned how long she could keep up the ruse of pretending to be in Greece though. She'd checked with the doorman at her mother's apartment building, and he'd confirmed that Angela had been home in Knightsbridge for a month. She wondered if perhaps her mother was jealous of her blossoming relationship with Grandy, even though she'd been the one to send Georgina to look after Eve. Georgina had often questioned if it was possible to hate your own mother as much as Angela seemed to hate hers. She certainly didn't hate Angela, but right now, she was finding it hard to like her. Angela Smytheson was an open book when it came to her selfishness and this behavior wasn't unusual, but Georgina for the first time saw what a truly unpleasant woman her mother could be.

After weeks of texting, phoning, and emailing, she'd finally managed to track her down. As Angela answered her phone Georgina could hear glasses clinking in the background and the sound of laughter. She now knew exactly where her mother was. Of course, she must be in her favorite haunt, in the bar at Harvey Nichols, with a glass of pinot noir and probably a plate of crudités. She knew it was her mother's golden rule to eat a little something when she drank, especially at four o'clock in the afternoon.

"Mum, why haven't you answered my texts or emails? I know you've been in London for a month. I found out when the cruise ended and Rick confirmed that you're back in your flat."

"I don't need you to tell me off. I can't even begin to tell you what a stressful time I've had, and I'm trying to relax before I come to see Grandy." .

"Stressful? Relax? You've been on a cruise. How stressful can that be? Don't you even want to know how Grandy is?"

"Oh, I'm sure you would have let me know if she'd died."

"What a horrible thing to say!"

"You know how much I hate that place, but I suppose I'll have to come and say my goodbyes to the old trout," Angela said, waving her empty glass at the bartender, indicating she wanted a refill. "Find me somewhere to stay nearby. I'm not staying in that dreadful house."

"You're impossible! There's no room for you here anyway. I'll book you into The Carpenters Arms around the corner. You'd better not let me down."

By four o'clock the following afternoon Angela had checked into the hotel. It was now four-thirty and she was sitting in the reception area, where she ordered a glass of wine and a selection of tea sandwiches from a young waitress dressed in black trousers and a crisp white blouse. She positioned herself so that she could see the comings and goings through the main door. She fidgeted nervously with the silk scarf around her neck as she waited for her daughter to arrive. A smartly dressed businessman turned to look appreciatively at her as he walked by. She wore a pale powder blue linen jacket over a simple black sheath dress. The blue of the jacket comple-mented her eyes; with her perfectly styled blonde hair and expertly Botoxed face she could easily pass for a much younger woman. She strummed her manicured fingernails on the arm of the chair; the crepey skin on the back of her hands was perhaps the only indication of her age.

"Mum—there you are! I've been up to your room looking for you. I didn't see you sitting there when I came in."

Georgina walked towards her, dressed in jeans, a pale pink sweater, and white trainers. She'd tied her long hair up in a high ponytail, and it swung from side to side playfully as she crossed the room. She looked almost like a teenager.

"You look different. Have you had a facelift?" Angela said, her eyes sweeping over her daughter. "Where have you been? I thought you'd be here by now. You know I don't like to be kept waiting."

"A facelift? Don't be ridiculous! I've been looking after Grandy. She's been telling me about her life in World War Two."

Georgina kissed her mother on both cheeks before perching on a leather armchair opposite her. There was a sudden flurry of activity. Someone had knocked a glass of wine off the table next to them and the waitress arrived with a cloth to mop it up. Georgina leaned forward in her chair to hear what her mother was saying.

"So, what secrets has my mother been telling you? Is it something about the sordid affair with a married man she had during the War?" Angela picked up a dainty cucumber sandwich and bit into it angrily.

"What do you mean 'sordid affair with a married man'? She was in France during the War. From what I can gather from her story so far, she met someone and fell in love."

"In France—don't be ridiculous. She worked as a nurse on the south coast somewhere, only she said it was top secret so she wouldn't have to tell us about her little affair. She managed to get herself into trouble, though. I dread to think who my father was."

"Well, that's not what she did. She was a secret agent for the Special Operations Executive. She went to Grenoble posing as a glovemaker."

"Oh, I really don't think so." After a couple of glasses of wine, Angela was now slurring her words. "She's never told me that. Mother, a secret agent—don't be silly! She would never have been capable of that. She's been watching too many of those war dramas on the TV. Talk about trying to reinvent history!"

"How much have you had to drink? I've never heard you be so nasty! You really don't care about Grandy, do you? You couldn't be bothered to break away from your holiday. I can't believe you still haven't asked how she is."

Angela played with the napkin on her lap. "How dare you accuse me of not caring!" she said. "That's a bit rich coming from you—you haven't been to see her for years! You have no idea what it was like for me growing up with her in that awful shop. You had a perfect childhood; just because you've roughed it for a few weeks you're suddenly a saint!"

Georgina's eyes widened in dismay as she listened to her mother rant on.

"I made sure you had the best of everything. And now you're turning on me. How dare you!"

Georgina and Eileen were in the kitchen the following morning when Angela knocked on the front door. Eileen was making the breakfast, as usual, and Georgina was sitting at the table eating a slice of toast. She was telling Eileen all about her mother's outburst.

"I'll go—it'll be her," she said glumly. She'd stayed longer than she wanted to with her mother the night before. The more Angela drank, the angrier she'd become. Georgina was exhausted and dreaded the impending reunion.

She found her mother on the doorstep clutching her over-size handbag. Angela breezed through the door, leaving a billow of cloying perfume in her wake. She glared at her daughter's flimsy nightie.

"Goodness me. Why aren't you dressed yet? Go upstairs and get some clothes on. Perhaps then we can get to the bottom of this fairytale you told me last night."

In her bedroom, Eve thought she heard raised voices. The sun was shining in through the open window, the warm morning air fanning her face. She had just hoisted herself up on her pillow when she heard knocking.

"May I come in, Mother?" Angela poked her head around the bedroom door.

"Angela! Is that really you? I thought you were in Greece or some such place—far too busy to bother with me."

Angela went over to her mother and planted a kiss on her cheek.

"It's lovely that you could find the time to come and see me," Eve said. "I thought that perhaps I would be gone by the time you got here."

"Don't be silly, Mum." Angela thrust her chin out defiantly. "Now—what's all this nonsense you've been filling Georgina's head with?"

"Nonsense? Someone needs to know, and as she was the only one who seemed interested...I did try to tell you about your father over the years, but you never wanted to listen. Your head was always in the clouds, planning some new adventure."

"If you think that this silly story of being a secret agent is somehow going to absolve you from being an awful mother to me, then think again. You were the little tart who came home from war pregnant. I only survived because of my grand-mother. You never told me the truth about my father because you were ashamed of the affair you had with a married man. You were ashamed that I was illegitimate!"

"What did you just call me? I can't believe you think of me like that! I've told you that your father was a special man because he was. Just knowing that he was in my life, that I was loved, even for such a brief time, has kept me going for all these years. You are the result of our love; how could I ever be ashamed of you? I'm sorry if you think I've been a bad mother."

Georgina, waiting outside the bedroom door, had heard the exchange and shook her head in disbelief. She knew that her mother could be selfish, but she had never heard her be so downright wicked before. She pushed the door open and took a deep breath.

"Why are you being so nasty? Grandy's not well."

Angela looked aghast at her daughter. "I still can't believe that you've been taken in by all this. She's never told me anything about what happened to her in the war, let alone being a secret agent. I remember it was my grandmother who told me that Grandy was a nurse in the Army and got herself pregnant by a married man. He didn't want anything to do with her after he found out she was expecting a baby. She told me that I was the result of that torrid affair. That's the real story."

She sat down heavily on the edge of the bed and shrugged off her coat.

"Yes, she told me something about a special love, but I've never believed that. And now she's adding some melodrama about being a secret agent in World War Two. I think maybe she has dementia."

Eve's eyes flashed angrily as she struggled to sit up. She leaned forward on one elbow.

"How dare you speak about me as if I'm not here. Dementia! I might be old but I'm not in the loony bin yet. Do you think that I never wanted you? Of course I wanted you. And if your father had lived to know you, he would have loved you as much as I do. I know you have always thought that I was a nurse during the war. That's what I led everyone to believe. I had no choice in the matter. I couldn't tell you what I did during the war; I'd sworn an oath of secrecy to the government." Eve gasped for breath and tears welled up in her eyes.

"Georgina now knows what really happened. All I have

169

ever wanted is to be a good mother to you, and you have always rejected me. I'm sorry Tom wasn't a nice man. I did my best to protect you." She fell back on the pillow, letting the tears flow down her cheeks. She fumbled for her oxygen mask. "Maybe you're right—maybe I was a bad mother."

Angela seemed unaware of her mother's obvious distress. She continued in her attack mode, years of pent-up vitriol spewing out.

"Well, if you must know, you didn't do enough. My childhood was horrible. It was bad enough that Tom was so unpleasant, but after you divorced him, people used to call me names. I was the pathetic girl with the weird mum who worked in a ghastly glove shop and was a tart. Everyone knew I was illegitimate. We never had enough money; nobody else's parents were divorced. I felt like an outcast. I couldn't wait to get out of here and make my own life. I would have loved a brother or sister to share things with. I was always alone."

"My goodness, I never knew how much you hated me. Is that what all this has been about? You've always felt sorry for yourself, haven't you? Why didn't you tell me what a terrible time you were having? I always knew you couldn't wait to get away from here though," Eve said sadly.

Georgina listened in dismay at her mother's outburst, worried for her grandmother's wellbeing. But her mother was relentless.

"I came here thinking that perhaps you wanted to make amends before you die. All I'm hearing are ridiculous excuses. Whatever you 'did' during the war doesn't make any difference to me now. I'm so happy I left this place. I just have to walk in through that front door to feel like I'm back in the nightmare." Angela's face was bright red and she was breathing fast.

Eve shrank into her bedcovers, her hands trembling as she reached for the oxygen mask.

"Perhaps you should leave. You're upsetting yourself and

me. I hope one day you'll find out who I am. I can only apologize again and again, but if you don't believe me, then there's no hope."

Angela opened her mouth to say something else, but Georgina stopped her. "I think you've said enough, Mum," she said. "You can believe what you want, but I know what Grandy has told me is true. There's nothing you can say that will make me change my mind. Grandy has been more of a family to me in the past few months than you've ever been. My childhood was no piece of cake either, if you must know. If you had spent enough time with me, perhaps I would have been able to tell you. I think she's right. You should go."

Georgina opened the bedroom door wide. She waited as her mother snatched her handbag off the bed before striding out of the room without saying goodbye to either of them. It wasn't until she heard the front door slam shut that she realized she hadn't told her about the baby.

CHAPTER 15

EVE
France, 1943

Despite her debilitating injury, Eve became increasingly anxious to secure her radio which she'd left hidden at the pension. She needed it in order to send the urgent message to London that they had been exposed and that the network was in jeopardy. She also fretted that someone might find it and that Mimi would be implicated. Eve suggested that Luc fetch it for her, but with deep snow on the ground, the only way he could reach Grenoble was on skis and he would almost certainly be stopped by *les Boches*. After considering the implications, they decided to leave the radio where it was. But Eve wasn't happy that she had to abandon her mission.

"I've let everyone down," she wailed. "I'm useless like this," she said hitting her leg angrily with her fist.

"There's nothing you can do. We're stuck in the mountains and the only way you can be safe is to hide for the near future. I'll have to return to my cadre soon. I could be punished for deserting."

"Thank you for staying here with me and looking after me," Eve said.

"I still have to get word to Madame Corot that her network has been exposed. If we can find somewhere safe for you to hide, then she should come too."

"Do you think she'll agree to that? She'll be concerned that you're involved."

"I know her—I'll persuade her to come, don't worry. I've heard of a farmer called Jacques who keeps a safe house for British airmen. He has a cave on his property which is used for aging cheese. There's a tunnel to it from inside one of his barns. It'll be the perfect hideout."

It came as a surprise to Eve that Madame Corot was hiding a Jewish mother and her little boy. The woman had taken them in during the round-up of Jews in Grenoble the previous year. Realizing that the pair would now be in even more jeopardy, Luc arranged for Madame Halévy and her son Jacob also to join them in their hideaway.

Luc and the other two women put what provisions they could muster in knapsacks, which they carried on their backs. Muffled in brightly colored woolen hats, scarves, and gloves, they looked like a group of tourists on a sightseeing trip in the Alps, when in fact they were fleeing for their lives. With Eve and the little boy settled on a sled, they set off further up the mountain. They followed a narrow road like a gash in the landscape, where they passed by houses built out of the rock of the mountainside. Nearing their destination in the late afternoon, they came to a village with just a *boulangerie* and a bar, the shutters of both firmly closed and unwelcoming. They continued along the main road for about two kilometers until they came to a small track lined with pine trees to their left, which took them deeper into the woods. When they could go no farther, they saw two long, stone-rendered buildings on either side of the track. At the very end, hidden from view, was the farmhouse. Calm and soothing farm noises of goats bleating and hens clucking came from inside one of the buildings. They turned to look at each other, relieved they had found a safe place to shelter. The front door opened and Monsieur Bizier shepherded them inside.

"We've been expecting you. I'm Jacques and this is my wife, Maude." Jacques Bizier nodded towards a pretty woman with dark, slightly graying hair, who was busying herself at a heavy black stove. "You're welcome to stay here for as long as you need to. Let's get this little angel out of the cold," he said, taking the sleeping toddler from Madame Halévy's arms. "When you've thawed yourselves out, we'll have dinner. I'm so happy you've come because my Maude has prepared her specialty—*un gratin dauphinois*. She's been saving the cheese for a special occasion, so you're very privileged, but it's my lucky day too. She used to feed me well once upon a time, but now I'm as thin as *un haricot vert!*" The gray-haired farmer laughed cheerily, slapping Luc on the back. Eve looked around her at the warm welcoming room and felt herself relax for the first time in days.

Maude's eyes lit up when she saw the little boy. Her arms reached out to him like a loving grandmother. The kitchen was warm and welcoming; the smell of potatoes, cheese, garlic, and cream baking in the oven made Eve's mouth water. It seemed like a miracle that Luc had found this haven for them amid so much turmoil. She shook off her heavy coat in happy anticipation of the meal to come.

Jacques by this time had opened a bottle of red wine and filled six rough tumblers that he'd taken from the pine dresser. Giving each of them a glass, he raised his in the air, giving a toast. "*Vive La France!*"

They all clinked glasses, drinking to each other. The wine was sharp and coated their teeth. Maude laid out the feast on the scrubbed kitchen table in front of them. As well as the promised *gratin*, she served thick slices of ham, braised cabbage, and apples scented with caraway seeds. The food and wine worked their magic, the atmosphere turning almost festive as the fugitives sat around chatting, enjoying each other's company, momentarily untroubled by life outside the small farmhouse. It was the nearest anyone had come to a celebration in a long time.

In the winter months in the mountains, when the snow piled up outside, Maude and Jacques busied themselves with inside work. Instead of the usual repair work that occupied their winter months, Maude now made little cardigans and leggings for Jacob, while Jacques started carving a wooden horse for the child. Eve and the two other women settled into a routine helping to cook, clean, and feed what few animals were left on the farm, and Maude taught Madame Halévy how to knit. It was a peaceful life, far from the wartime horrors occurring just a few miles away.

Her first days at the farm were the happiest of Eve's life. Luc had cleared an area in one of the outbuildings next to the barn, where she would be able to work out once her bone was healed. Each morning, he carried her there from the barn and demonstrated what she would need to do to strengthen her leg muscles. It really was more of an excuse to be alone together, though, as it would be several weeks before she would be able to put weight on her leg. Eve treasured those days she spent with him. She loved the feel of his strong arms around her and the gentleness with which he took care of her. He did teach her some exercises, but mostly they spent time sharing their hopes and dreams for the future. The electricity that was present between them when they first met became even stronger. He told her he was in awe of her, not just of her prettiness, but of her determination and strength, and she in turn basked in his admiration. It was as if they were always meant to be together.

Then, two weeks after their arrival, Luc gently told Eve that he would have to rejoin his cadre lower in the mountains ten miles away. He didn't know when he would be able to return. She felt miserable. In their brief time together, they had fallen in love. She was scared for his safety, and her heart ached in a way she had never felt before; loving him made her feel vulnerable. Still grieving for Sylvie, she found the possibility of also losing Luc terrifying. She was fearful too that her important line of communication with the SOE had been cut. Her mission was in jeopardy. Frustration and heartache mingled in her young head, and the pain in her leg was a constant reminder of her inability to do her job.

After Luc had left, it was Madame Corot who supervised Eve as she did the exercises that Luc had taught her, making sure that she made no mistakes that could jeopardize her recovery.

"You can call me Arlette," the woman said one day. I'm only a few years older than you. 'Madame' makes me feel ancient. We've been together now for weeks—it's not like we don't know each other. We depend on each other, and you've become a good friend."

"You're right. It does sound a bit ridiculous after all we've been through," Eve said. "I can't thank you enough for all the support you're giving me."

But much as she needed a friend, she knew she would never be able to share the secret of her identity with the woman. Sylvie and her uncle were the only ones who knew. She hadn't even told Luc.

Spring came at last. Outside in the mountains, they could hear the drip-drip of the thawing ice. But high up, the ground was surprisingly dry. The meltwater had already found its way into cracks in the limestone, disappearing through the rocks to underground waterways and caves deep within the mountainside.

Now that it was warmer, Eve wanted more than anything to be outdoors and to be able to walk without the use of her stick. Jacques had crafted a special one for her, carving the handle in the shape of an eagle's head, and had measured it exactly to accommodate her height. But despite its beauty and utility, the stick made her feel like an old woman.

One afternoon in late May, Eve was alone in the barn when she heard a tapping on the heavy pine door. She hoisted herself to her feet, limping awkwardly to see who it was. She heard a whisper.

"Eve, it's me, Luc. Arlette told me you were here by yourself."

The door creaked open, and Luc walked in. The sun shining through a window high in the wall of the barn danced on Eve's hair as she looked up at him. They stared at each other for a full minute before either of them moved. She shuffled towards him, almost falling into his arms.

"I have been so worried about you," she said.

"Thinking about you is the only thing that has kept me going. I missed you and I needed to see how you are. I shouldn't be here though. They could shoot me for deserting."

Watching him rub his hand over the dark stubble of his beard, her knees started to tremble. "You've risked getting into trouble just to see me? Oh, Luc, I've missed you so much! What's going on out there?"

"There's twenty of us now in my cadre. Finally, we have guns and explosives to work with. This week we sabotaged the ammunition depot outside Grenoble with a group of Communists. We also blew up two bridges to slow down the German advance. But it's not been without retaliation from *les Boches*. Six men and two women were taken from Collard and shot. It's terrible. I keep wondering if it's worth it."

"More reprisals. That's awful!"

"And rumor has it we're expected to go into combat. We won't stand a chance. Most of us don't know how to use the weapons we've been given. We've no defense training—I'm a doctor, for God's sake; I'm supposed to keep people alive, not kill them. But the only chance we have now is to chip away at the bastards bit by bit, with all the pain it entails."

She squeezed his hand. "Do you know any of the people who were killed?"

"Unfortunately, I do." The dark circles under his eyes added to his overall look of sadness. "Can we just forget about it all for now? What have you been doing?" he asked, caressing her cheek with his thumb.

"I should be out there helping—it's been so quiet here and I feel so useless and guilty. The others spend most of the daylight hours in the farmhouse, but I've kept myself busy doing this." She pointed to a table where glove halves lay like a series of handprints. Luc picked up a pair of pale pink gloves, touching the softness of the leather with his rough hands.

"These are beautiful— you really are a glovemaker, aren't you."

"I made them a while ago. I'm saving them for when I get married one day."

"Well, we'll have to see how we can make that happen," he whispered so quietly that she wondered if she'd imagined it.

She felt her heart flutter again. Suddenly nothing else mattered in the world except being with him.

"I can't believe I feel like this, and I know so little about you," he said.

Eve knew that she could never reveal her identity. It was against all the rules. She hesitated, before telling him a concoction of truth and lies, hating herself for doing it.

"What more do you want to know? You already know I come from Paris, where my family were glovemakers, and that my mother is no longer alive. You know that I am an only child too. What else? — I love fashion. My favorite color is pink. I can't play a musical instrument, although I have always wanted to play the piano. I have the most terrible singing voice. I'm afraid of the dark and I'm in love with you—I've never felt more certain about anything."

"I've been thinking about doing this for days. I can't help it—I love you too." Bending down, he put his lips on hers and kissed her slowly as he slipped his hands under her blouse, gently running them over the soft skin of her rib cage, until his thumbs reached the swell of her breasts. She let out a soft moan, not wanting him to stop, and pressed her body against his. He swung her into his arms before carrying her over to a deep pile of hay in the corner of the barn, where he gently lay her down.

The weeks dragged on and Eve's leg slowly became stronger. Luc visited several times, but always at night and never for long. The stories he brought with him were frightening ones of more reprisals and arrests. It wasn't an ordinary courtship; the fleeting hours they spent together were intense and passionate. But it was hard to have a carefree love affair. Mixed emotions played games in her head. She and Sylvie had both been warned of the risks of their mission, but she never imagined things would turn out the way they had. She felt guilty that she was no longer able to undertake what she'd been sent to do, and she worried constantly about her uncle and friends.

"I hope you'll wait for me and not go back to Paris when the War is over—I don't want to lose you. I can't imagine living my life without you."

"Oh Luc, I could never leave you. I have no plans to go back to Paris. When this is all over, I want to be with you forever."

Eve lay next to him on their makeshift bed in the barn. She turned sideways and ran her fingers over his chest, loving the warmth of his skin next to hers, wondering how it was possible to have found such happiness and love amid all the horror and pain. She studied every inch of him, taking pictures of him in her mind, storing them for eternity.

"I still can't believe that you're working for the Resistance. You could have been a glovemaker and not risked your life. I'm glad that you broke your leg. At least now you're safe. If anything happens to you like your friend Sylvie..."

Eve squeezed her eyes shut. It was too painful to think about Sylvie.

"*Ma chérie*," he said. "I can't wait to spend the rest of my life with you. I've never met anyone like you before—so beautiful and gentle, strong and brave." She opened her eyes as he took her face in his two hands. "I want to remember this moment forever," he whispered.

"Wherever you are, my darling, just know that you'll always be in my heart," Eve softly replied.

The morning light was pushing its way in through the cracks in the shutters. It had been a hot night, not unusual for early July, and none of the women had slept that well. They were already up when they heard Jacques shouting outside the barn door. Eve opened the door to look outside. The sun was slowly rising, like a balloon floating on the horizon, turning the sky red and ominous. Jacques was having trouble getting his words out fast enough.

"I was in the village. I saw two cars coming in the distance—it's *les Boches*. They're coming! They must be trying to surprise us. Quick as you can, get into the tunnel and I'll cover the trapdoor. Follow the instructions we've rehearsed, and you'll be fine. Things are heating up and the Allies are making a move. There is news that they've landed in the south and the German army is retreating. Hurry!"

In the distance, they could hear the grating of gears as the vehicles climbed the mountain road. They didn't have long to escape, but were well prepared, having practiced a quick getaway many times.

"I've got Jacob," Eve said as she grabbed her bag and slung it over her shoulder. She picked up the child's bottle that had been left lying on the table.

"Come on," she said calmly to the boy. "Let's play hide and go seek." Moving as fast as she could on her broken leg, she took him by the hand and led him to the trap door. She dropped her heavy bag down into the tunnel first, and then gingerly lowered herself onto the ladder, wincing in pain on each rung, before reaching up and lifting Jacob to safety.

The two other women moved fast. They ran back to the farmhouse taking with them any evidence of their presence in the barn. Then they joined Eve and Jacob in the underground hideout. By the time the cars pulled into the farmyard, the women and the child were safely hidden. Jacques, as planned, had placed a hopper containing grain for the goats over the entrance to the cave, and was outside in the yard pumping water into a bucket from the well when the Germans got out of their cars.

"We have reason to believe that you have been helping enemy airmen to escape. Our informants tell us that you are part of the Resistance network. You'd be surprised how much information we get out of your stupid people with a little pressure."

A gold tooth glistened menacingly in the officer's mouth.

"There was a lovely young thing that I had some fun with only last week—she squealed quickly."

Jacques looked into the man's eyes, thinking that if the Devil lived, then he'd just met him. Glowering at him he said, "I don't know what you think you will find here—you're welcome to look. It's early. Not even my wife is up yet."

One of the soldiers was already in the barn, sticking his bayonet into sacks of potatoes piled up against a wall. Another had climbed into the hayloft, kicking and stomping in his booted feet across the floor, straw flying in all directions, enraged that he couldn't find anything. The officer lit a cigarette, throwing the match onto the floor of the barn. "Well, this should smoke them out."

He frog-marched Jacques outside, leaving the door open behind him. As the outside air flowed into the space, a huge explosion of fire ignited the hayloft and everything went red.

The soldiers took their time going through the rest of the farm, enjoying the fear and horror on Jacques's face, as they ripped the place apart. Finding no one, they set everything alight.

Seeing Jacques's wife open the door to the farmhouse, the officer walked towards her, undoing his belt, loosening the waistband of his trousers. "Well, while we're waiting for them to come out of their hiding hole, we may as well have some fun," he said. "Your wife might even enjoy this. Most women do." The officer hit her hard across the face. She crumpled to the ground in terror. The painful sound of Jacques's keening voice echoed around the farmyard.

In the cavern underneath the mountain, unaware of what was happening, the women waited. It was difficult to assess how much time passed except that they had burned through almost one candle. They made themselves as comfortable as they could, but in the limestone cave, it was cold. A couple of blankets used by previous escapees were still there, and they huddled together, glad of each other for comfort and warmth.

At the beginning of the war, Jacques helped a friend hide his precious wine collection. Hearing that the Germans were confiscating fine Beaujolais from nearby vineyards, the vintner transported his best vintages to Jacques's cave for safekeeping. Racks containing the bottles ran along one wall. As their eyes became accustomed to the dimness, the women could make out another wooden rack where cheeses were traditionally stored while they matured. There was nothing there now except for a few apples, potatoes, a couple of jars of pickled vegetables, and a bag of walnuts.

Eve's frustration was bubbling over.

"What are we going to do? We need to find out what's happening, and I'm no good to anyone."

The hours of confinement had made her leg become swollen and stiff.

"Don't worry—I'll go and see what's going on. I think Jacques said that there's a rock in the ceiling that can be removed. Perhaps I can see through," Arlette said. "I'm sorry, but I'll have to leave you in the dark. I'll come back to fetch you if I think it looks safe." Eve trembled as Arlette disappeared down the short tunnel carrying the remaining candle. She was terrified of the blackness and clutched Madame Halévy's hand.

"Do you think there are bats down here? she said. "I don't think I can stay here if there's no light. I hope Arlette comes back soon." She closed her eyes and started to count slowly to calm herself. It was a trick she'd learned in training, and she hoped that it would work.

After what seemed like hours to Eve, but was only minutes, Arlette returned. Eve opened her eyes and was relieved to see that the candle was still burning.

"Thank goodness you're back. Have the Germans left?"

"It looks as if they have. I think it's safe to leave."

The two women and the little boy made their way out of

the cave, down the tunnel and up the ladder to the trapdoor, guided by Arlette who was still clutching the flickering candle.

Together Arlette and Madame Halévy partially moved the burnt-out grain hopper and squeezed their way through a small opening, before helping Jacob and then Eve to get out. It was deathly quiet outside in the yard. Billows of thick choking smog wafted from the smoldering buildings, making it difficult to breathe. Looking around for any sign of life, they saw a goat stumbling through the charred ruins, its kid following closely behind. The bodies of Jacques and his wife lay on different sides of the burnt-out yard. Their throats were cut. They stood in shock with their hands over their mouths. Madame Halévy held Jacob close to her chest, shielding him from the horror in front of their eyes.

As they looked in terror at the dreadful scene, a man's figure emerged from the smoky shadows on the other side of the farmyard. Gruppenführer Müller strolled nonchalantly toward them. He and his soldiers were still there.

"What do we have here? We've been waiting for you. We were expecting to smoke out some British airmen, not women and children. That stupid man was hiding Jews—but I'm not sure about you. I haven't seen many blonde Jews." He seized Arlette by her hair. Then he put his first two fingers in his mouth and whistled. Two soldiers came running. "It's your lucky day. This is better than the airmen we were hoping to find," he said. "Take your pick—but I'm having her." He kept hold of Arlette's hair and dragged her into the woods.

"I'm taking the one with the child," one of the soldiers declared. He looked down at Eve's leg. "I don't want to screw a cripple."

The little boy started to scream as the soldier pulled his mother away, wrenching his little hand from her grip. Eve made a move towards Jacob as the third soldier towered over her. She held her cane tightly, unsure if she could use it to defend herself if the opportunity arose. Then the German made a show of grabbing her hand, taking the stick off her, and dragging her into the woods away from the others. She stumbled alongside him, terrified of what would happen to the little boy who was now alone in the yard. The knife she had hidden in her sock dug into her ankle as the soldier pulled her along. But she knew that she was overpowered and that she wouldn't be able to use her training against the large man. Terror and anger boiled up inside her and she feared the worst as the man pushed her down on a fallen tree trunk. He balanced alongside her, still holding her tightly so that she couldn't escape. But now that she looked at him more closely, she could see that he was younger than her, and he appeared oddly vulnerable. His eyes were sad, and his dirty blonde hair hung limply on his forehead. He hung his head and seemed to hesitate as he let go of her arm. Her heart thumped painfully in her chest, and she thought for a moment that perhaps she had a chance to kill him. She inched her hand slowly towards her sock, feeling for the knife's handle. She was finding it hard to breathe when she heard the man speak in faltering English.

"I don't want to hurt you—I just want to go home and see my mother and my sisters again. I hate this war—I hate those men," he said, nodding over to the other side of the woods. "It's over anyway. We won nothing." He looked down at his boots, not able to look her in the eye, his face full of despair, tears trembling on his thick white eyelashes. "Please go and take the child with you," he begged her. "I'll say I killed you both."

"What about my friends?" A groan escaped from her throat as her question trickled out.

The young soldier shook his head sadly. Eve squeezed his arm and got up. He nodded. She hobbled towards the sound of Jacob's wails, leaving the young man sobbing quietly behind her.

CHAPTER 16

EVE
France, 1944

The village near the farmhouse looked like a burnt-out shell, the scars of bullets pock-marking the walls of the stone buildings. There was a sickly-sweet smell of burnt flesh in the air, the silence broken only by birdsong and unoiled shutters creaking back and forth in the wind. Eve stumbled along, holding the child's hand, until she reached the church on the outskirts of the village. It was burned to the ground. She did her best to block her imagination from telling her what had happened, but waves of dizziness and nausea washed over her as she tried to breathe in the torrid air, and she vomited at the side of the road. She picked up the boy, making her way through the graveyard and out of the village. Progress was slow as they made their way down the mountainside, the ground now becoming softer under her feet. Carrying Jacob was hard, but at least he hadn't made a sound since they had left the farmhouse. Finally exhausted, she settled him down next to the trunk of a tree and they both slept.

They carried on for days with little to eat except for berries she picked and the handful of walnuts that she had found in her bag, stopping only when darkness fell. That she was still alive, while everyone around her was dead, was unbearable to think about; images of Jacques and Maude, each lying in a pool of blood, flashed in front of her eyes. The hope of finding Luc and her uncle alive and the need to get the child to safety were all that kept her going.

One day, stopping at a vantage point behind a rocky ridge, she could see activity far in the distance. She was unsure what to do. She put the boy down on the ground. Through the canopy of billowing pine trees, she saw thick smoke pluming in the air from a town she believed she had once been through. It was where she thought Luc and his group of *maquisards* were in hiding. She felt Jacob tugging at her skirt, wanting to be picked up. Scooping him into her arms, she limped doggedly towards the town, drawn by a thin strand of hope.

The sun was starting to set in the sky. Following a path through the woods, she came across a stream, alongside which a covey of ptarmigan was searching for insects and lichen on the forest floor, and clumps of white anemones lay like soft pillows inviting them to rest. The birds paid them no attention, intent on foraging for their own survival. The bleating of goats calling to each other in the distance echoed through the trees and the low whir of crickets was rising into a crescendo. Removing her shoes, she dangled her feet in the ice-cold water, letting it relax her aching legs. She dipped the toddler's bottle into the stream to fill it for him. He sucked thirstily, self-soothing as he laid his head on her knee. In the hot and sultry air, tiny flies buzzed annoyingly around the child's head as she absent-mindedly swatted them with her hand. Then she heard a faint sound, almost a whisper. Looking up, she saw a face on the other side of the stream.

It was someone she recognized: Albert, the man who met them when they had first arrived in France. He didn't move but seemed to be trying to tell her something. His eyes darted from side to side. He motioned with his hand for them to stay still. She didn't speak as she slowly lifted her legs out of the water. The child had fallen asleep. She gently transferred his head from her knee to the ground. Albert waded silently across the water towards her. He stopped right next to her and whispered into her ear.

"*Les Boches* are close by," he said, his breath stale and hot. "You have to hide—now!" There was a desperation in his voice that scared her. He gripped her arm, dragging her with him.

"Please, I can't go any faster," she whispered. "The child..."

He paid her no heed, pulling her with the sleeping child in her arms. She heard a dog bark and the sound of a whistle.

"Do you have a gun?" he whispered.

"No, just a knife. But I know how to use it." The blood drained from her face and her head went woozy.

"You may well have to, but there are only two of them with a dog. I'll double back and try to put the dog off our scent."

He pushed her toward a dense thicket. "Hide in there until I return." He ran off, leaving her alone with the child.

She waited and waited. A gunshot sounded in the distance. Her knife felt cold in her pocket. Then she heard footsteps coming closer and, peering through the bushes, saw a pair of military jackboots. The air was very still. She was sure that the soldier would hear her breathing. He sat down on the ground just feet from where she was hiding. He reached in his pocket for a cigarette and lit it. The now-familiar aromatic smoke floated towards them. The child coughed in his sleep. The German turned and their eyes met. She clutched at the damp handle of the dagger and a trickle of sweat ran down her face.

Eve realized that if she was going to kill him, then this was the moment to do it. As she was about to lunge, she heard a gunshot. A look of surprise came over the soldier's face as he slumped forward, falling almost on top of her. Albert stood in the clearing. He took off his beret and used it to wipe his face. He spat on the ground.

"One fewer of the bastards for us to deal with," he said dispassionately. "I got the other one and the dog too." He took out a cigarette and lit it. They sat in silence, the dead body lying beside them. Eve hugged the child close.

They had been sitting without saying a word for some time when they heard a twig snap.

"Don't move," a voice growled. A man seemed to float out of the shadows of the trees like a ghost. He was unshaven and dirty, but despite his deeply lined and weathered face, Eve realized that he was young. He wore a raincoat that was far too big for his skinny body. He carried a pistol in each hand, poking out from the sleeves of the overlarge coat. He glided towards them, his eyes briefly wandering over the dead soldier.

"You should be careful—the Allies have started their advance from the south. The entire German army is moving north. There are thousands of them—they've been torching towns and villages as they leave. I've come from Vassieux. They burned it to the ground. They murdered women and children and hanged their husbands and fathers in the street. We were helpless to stop them—don't go anywhere near there." His hollow eyes looked dead. "The smell of smoldering bodies is something I will never be able to forget."

He collapsed to his knees in front of Eve. She felt for his hand and squeezed it. She pulled him towards her. The brittleness of his skeletal body shocked her. She knew that there was nothing she could say that would possibly comfort him. Her only thoughts were of Luc and his comrades who had been hiding in and near Vassieux. "Is there anyone left alive?" Her heart thumped painfully in her chest as her question hovered in the air between them. Looking at the despair in his eyes, she didn't need to wait for the answer.

"My wife!" Albert yelled. "I have to find her." He went over to the dead soldier, took the man's gun out of its holster, and ran into the forest.

For the next two days, the young man traveled with them; she leaned against his fragile body as he carried the boy, sharing a bond of pain and what little food they had between them. When they reached the outskirts of Grenoble, he turned to her.

"I must go home to find out what's happened to my family—take this." He gave her one of the pistols. "I don't need it anymore. Good luck." He turned and slowly walked up a track towards his house, his tattered coat dragging in the dirt behind him.

In the distance, she could see French flags flying from buildings in the city. Grenoble had been liberated.

As they picked their way through the rubble, Eve witnessed a group of men dragging a girl along by her legs. She pushed Jacob's head into her shoulder so that he couldn't see.

"*Putain!* You deserve to die for collaborating with *les Boches.* You're a filthy whore!" a partisan shouted.

The girl's eyes were wide open with fear, her head shaved, blood pouring from a gash on her face. The space that surrounded the men exuded a ferocity that was horribly triumphant. Their hatred and cruelty made Eve feel queasy. She staggered with the weight of the little boy in her arms to the other side of the bridge, not wanting to be part of the thuggish justice, nor wanting to see what they would do next to the accused woman.

Someone had pulled chairs onto the street outside *La Ganterie Dupuis*. Most of them were hacked to pieces. The main doors to the building creaked backwards and forwards, the hollow sound reflecting Eve's own feeling of emptiness and desolation.

"I have to go inside and look for someone," she said to Jacob. "You must stay here and be a good boy." She lifted him up, sitting him on the only undamaged chair she could find. "I won't be long."

The child looked up at her. He put his thumb in his mouth, sucking it patiently, his breathing soft and even, unlike her own. His eyes were so trusting, they made her want to weep.

She cautiously made her way into the hallway, where papers were strewn over the floor and swastikas screamed angrily from the walls. Hearing a moaning sound coming from the office, she felt for the security of the gun in her pocket. She put her ear against the closed door. She listened for a while before turning the doorknob to look inside. What met her eyes was a disaster. Records of her uncle's business were senselessly tossed about, and his desk, a family heirloom, had been destroyed. Thinking that the noise she heard must have come from outside in the street, she turned to leave; then she noticed what looked to be a bundle of old clothes behind a chair. It was moving up and down very slowly. Her heart pounded painfully in her chest. She carefully took the gun out of her pocket, unsure of what she would do, but ready for anything. Not wanting to get too close, she kicked the heap tentatively with her foot. A hand sprang out from under the rags, batting her away and causing the rags to fall to one side.

"Oh my God, Celeste," Eve smiled, happy to at last see a familiar face. "Is that really you?"

Two beady eyes peered out at her from a head that was completely bald. Then, Eve's mind flashed back to the bridge where she had seen the partisans dragging the woman just minutes earlier. It took her an instant to fully grasp what Celeste had done.

"Of course, it was you! You betrayed everyone collaborating with *les Boches*. And I thought that they had broken Jules. Bertrand knew there was a spy in the network, but you were the last person he would have expected to betray him."

Eve couldn't help but notice that the woman's flabby face looked fatter than before, now that she no longer had any hair. "You never went hungry like the rest of us, did you," Eve sneered, feeling angrier than she ever had in her life.

"You didn't think I'd guess who you were—stupid girl!" Celeste lisped, blood dribbling through her broken teeth. "I knew from the moment I saw you. And if you thought I believed that cock and bull story you told me about Sylvie going home to Paris, I'm not an idiot! We were managing all right without the British interfering in our affairs. If Bertrand had just worked with *les Allemandes* like I told him to, life would have gone on as usual."

"You deserve what the partisans have done to you! Where are my friends and my uncle?"

"They're all dead. They took their time with Bertrand. He was hanged in La Place Grenette—it took him hours to die. They brought your aunt to watch."

"Is she still alive?"

"Of course not. They killed her too."

Eve was appalled by Celeste's dispassion at her uncle's death, but she said nothing. She stared ahead, unable to look at the fat woman, clenching her fists tightly, torn between the mounting urge to slap her hard and the revulsion of touching her. "What about Marie, Sandrine, and the others?"

"I told you, they're all dead. The Germans killed everyone they held prisoner just before they retreated."

"And you did nothing to stop them from killing our friends? They weren't part of any network; they knew nothing about our work. You evil bitch—I always knew you were an unpleasant woman, but I would never have thought you capable of this. But there's something I don't understand. Why didn't you tell *la Milice* where I was hiding that day?"

"I thought they had already taken you outside," Celeste said sullenly. "I thought I saw them put you in the truck."

Eve finally squeezed the handle of the gun and readied herself. She pointed it at Celeste. Her finger was itching to pull the trigger and put a bullet in the woman's head. She paused for a moment, until she couldn't resist the impulse any longer. Just as Celeste began to stand up, Eve lifted the barrel of the gun and pointed it in her direction. Celeste swayed, a look of horror on her face, and fell back. Eve pulled the trigger once and then again, and again, energized by the satisfaction the action gave her. She kept on shooting until there were no bullets left. When she had finished, she tossed the empty gun over to where Celeste was cowering in terror. "Take it. You're not worth killing. You're worth nothing."

Outside the streets were overflowing with people—soldiers, men, women, and children dancing and hugging each other. Jacob lay curled up on the chair where she had left him. She reached for him and took him in her arms. "I have one more place to go," she said, more to herself than to the child. His little arms and legs clung to her.

When she came to La Place Grenette, she saw even more signs of destruction everywhere. Chairs and tables from Monsieur Duron's bar had been used to break the windows of neighboring businesses, and the door to Chez Mimi was smashed in. The surrounding buildings were riddled with bullet holes, shutters hanging in windows like pages half torn from a book, dangling uselessly.

Pulled by a now fraying thread of hope, she carefully eased

herself through a gap in the familiar green door. She called out, half expecting to hear Mimi's voice. Inside it was eerily quiet, contrasting with the laughter and cheering coming from outside in the street; someone started to play an accordion, the music filling the square with a jaunty mood, so at odds with the picture in front of her. Meaningless destruction again met her. She climbed the steep staircase to the room she had shared with Sylvie, where she found their clothes strewn across the floor, the furniture smashed. Outside, across the square, people were dancing for joy and children were splashing in the fountain. Tears blurred her vision and she thought she saw Jules. She looked again, but he was gone. She had no idea where she would go, but knew she had to get the child to safety. She had never felt so alone.

The stairs seemed steeper than before. Her legs ached. She sat down and shuffled down step by step on her bottom until she reached the foyer. The sound of footsteps coming from the kitchen startled her. Suddenly her heart thumping painfully in her chest seemed to stop; she finally succumbed to what her body had been telling her to do for days. Everything went black as she hit the stone floor.

When she came to, Jules was leaning over her with a cold damp cloth in his hand. Her breath came in ragged bursts.

"Where am I? You're dead. Where's Jacob?" The thought occurred to her that she may have died too, and that she was in some sort of halfway house, where God decided what to do with you.

"Nothing can keep a good man down," he said grimly. "Luckily I managed to escape before the Gestapo got hold of me—I've been hiding ever since. I came to look for you, Sylvie, and Bertrand. Who's Jacob?"

"He's a little boy I'm looking after. They raped and then killed his mother. Sylvie's dead and so are Bertrand and the others—it was Celeste who was the traitor." Her words sounded hollow and flat. She didn't even recognize her own voice as she said in English, "I want to go home to England."

"What did you say? England!" he exclaimed, understanding the words she uttered. "You're British?"

"I'm an agent with the SOE and so was Sylvie. We lost our war—nothing went our way."

"You're wrong—we've won the War. France is free."

Eve clung onto him like the lifeline she'd needed for days. "What was it all for? Too many people have died," she sobbed. "I've lost everything and everyone I loved here—I didn't help anyone."

"Come with me to America, to Hollywood. I'm going to start a new life where there are no memories of what we've been through. One day I'll be a famous actor," he said, seemingly unfazed by what he had seen and done.

For the first time in days, she heard the small boy cry out. She got up, following the sound of his sobbing. He crouched in the corner of the hallway.

"I must get him somewhere safe," she said as she collapsed on the floor next to him.

Gradually Jules coaxed her to stand, picking up the child in his arms. He found a table at the bistro on the corner, where a man offered them bowls of watery soup and a hunk of bread. Eve gave the boy the broth and most of her bread.

As they sat there eating, Jules gently told her what had happened to their Resistance network and to the partisans in the Vercors. But the story he told her was heartbreaking.

The Allies had landed in southern France and, with the help of the Resistance, had managed to defeat the German army's position, forcing them to withdraw north through the Rhône Valley. The Resistance did everything in their power to impede their retreat, and they in part succeeded. After the Normandy landings, the paramilitary groups of the Resistance became more organized, enabling the Free French Forces of the Interior to liberate Grenoble. But it all came at great cost to the city and to the towns and villages in the German army's wake. They burned Vassieux to the ground and murdered its villagers. Before they abandoned the city six days after the Provence landings, they massacred every prisoner they'd previously held captive. They had killed over eight hundred residents during their occupation.

She stared into space as he spoke, listening to what she didn't want to hear. "This wasn't how it was meant to turn out," she wept.

"Come," he said. "Let's get you home."

CHAPTER 17

GEORGINA AND EVE
England, 2016

Georgina glanced at her watch. Paul was half an hour late and the meal that she'd ordered was already sitting on the table.

He arrived, very flustered.

"Sorry I'm late. There was something that I wanted to verify before I put everything together for you. I've found out quite a lot of information." He sat next to her on the bench.

"What's all this?" he asked, pointing to the food set out in front of him.

"I just want to say thank you," Georgina said. "I hope you don't mind me ordering for you."

Paul looked at the array of dishes. "That's very kind of you," he said. "You didn't need to do that, but I am hungry. I haven't stopped all day." He spooned the curry and then rice on his plate and started to eat. He'd only taken a couple of bites when his face turned red like a beetroot, with drops of perspiration trickling down his face. He started to cough and couldn't stop.

"Are you okay?"

"Mmm... Give me a minute." He blew his nose loudly, honking like a goose. "It's really hot. I don't think I can manage anymore. I'm not too good with chicken vindaloo."

"Why on earth are you eating it then?"

"I didn't want you to think I was a wimp." He wiped his face with his napkin and took a big gulp of water.

She burst out laughing. "You idiot! I'm flattered you wanted to impress me, though." She handed him a piece of naan. "Here, eat this, it'll take the heat away."

Paul chewed on the bread and sniffed loudly.

"Oh, it's one of those manly things we men do when we like someone." He took off his glasses and rubbed his watery eyes. He reached down for his backpack and took out a folder. "So, here's the scoop. I've found birth, baptism, and marriage records for a man named Luc Gaspard. But there's no death certificate documented. He was married in 1953, had a son named Jean Luc who was born in 1955, and his wife passed away in 1991."

"So, it's possible that Luc Gaspard could still be alive?"

"Yes, but he could be dead too. He would be ninety-four now."

"What do we do next?"

"Well, if you like, I can try contacting Jean-Luc Gaspard, his son. He must be in his sixties. I think we should start in the same town where Luc originally lived. If he doesn't live there, it's going to be a process of elimination until we find him. It could be like looking for a needle in a haystack."

Georgina took a slow sip of her drink. "Poor Grandy! She's lived her life pining for someone who could still be alive. What a waste."

"Perhaps we can rectify things before it's too late. Maybe she will get to see him again."

"Oh, do you really think so? But I'm not going to say a

word of any of this to her just yet. I don't want to get her hopes up."

As she listened to Paul talk more about his plan to find her grandfather, she noticed again how handsome he was when he became animated. She was puzzled how she had ever thought him boring; there was something about his voice that was solid and dependable, that made her feel safe. Yes, he was a bit scruffy, but it somehow made him more endearing, like a puppy in need of rescuing. And he'd just said he liked her.

"How do you think we should go from here?" she asked.

"Well, if I am able to locate Luc's son, perhaps we could go to France and talk to him in person."

"We? Do you mean you would come with me?"

"Of course. It would be my pleasure. I love this kind of thing."

"It'll be so amazing if we can find him, and I'd get to spend some time alone with you too. I'd love to get to know you better," she said.

Paul coughed again as he nervously shoved his paperwork into his backpack.

"You're really going to go to France with Paul?" Camilla asked.

Georgina glowed now that she'd started to get over her morning sickness. Camilla thought she'd never seen her look happier, and there was a softness about her that made her look even more beautiful.

"Yes. He's been so lovely and helpful. He's taking care of all the travel arrangements. Can you believe it? I haven't told Grandy yet, but if we find Luc, I hope he'll be fit enough to travel here to see her. I'm not sure we could get her to France. I won't surprise her though—the shock might be too much!"

"So, is there anything you should tell me about you and Paul?"

"I really like him. I'm surprised how well we get on together. But I must be losing my touch. He doesn't seem that interested in me."

"Matt says that he said he's smitten with you."

"Is he really 'smitten' with me?" Georgina wondered out loud.

"It would seem so! Does he know you're pregnant? How are you feeling, by the way? You look wonderful. Did you see the doctor?"

"I had an ultrasound and I'm twelve weeks. Everything looks good."

"Is it a boy or a girl?"

"It's a girl." Georgina grinned. "So much has happened since I left New York. I have another person growing inside me." She caressed her belly with a wondrous look in her eyes.

"So, does your grandmother know yet?"

"Yes, she does. We had a long chat about it. She's made me feel much more confident about everything. I can do this! She's been so encouraging and not at all judgmental. She told me the same as you, I should tell Marco about the baby, and I agree. He has every right to be in her life, but I know I'm lucky that I can afford to bring her up by myself. I'm really surprised how much I want her. My grandmother has made me feel part of a real family. I'm going to make sure that my little girl knows what that feels like. But there's so much going on. Now I don't know what I'm more excited about— trying to find my grandfather or having a baby."

Camilla hugged her friend tight. "All I know, Georgie, is that when you're around, it's never dull!"

Paul's lengthy searches had revealed that Jean-Luc Gaspard from Grenoble had a father named Luc who had fought with the Resistance during World War Two. Luc was alive. After the war ended, he continued with his medical studies. He had been a doctor in the small town of Saint-Nizier-du-Moucherotte for his entire life.

Sitting next to Paul on the Air France flight to Grenoble the following week, Georgina couldn't help but think about how her brave little grandmother must have felt over seventy years before. She wondered how different the view from her window was compared to the terrain in 1943. The mountain peaks of the Alps were covered with a smattering of snow. The broad riverbeds that pilots used to chart their way during World War Two were still there; tributaries spread out like fingers of a hand.

She looked up and saw that the seat belt sign had just been switched on. She felt for her belt to tighten it. Paul looked over at her.

"Nervous?" he asked.

"Yes, I am a little bit. What if he doesn't like me?"

"If I know you, you'll win him over. Not long now," he said. "We'll check into the hotel in Grenoble later tonight. I've booked two rooms for us at the Le Grand Hotel."

"You didn't need to splash out on two rooms. I don't mind doubling up if you don't," Georgina said suggestively.

"Smytheson, you're a terrible flirt. I've never met anyone quite like you."

"What do you mean?"

"I mean I've never been attracted to anyone like you before and you're driving me crazy. Can you please just shut up and let me make the moves!"

"You know, I've never been attracted to anyone like you either. At first, I thought you were a boring old fart, with an excellent taste in fancy cars, but you've grown on me."

"Thanks a lot!"

"No, what I mean is I really like you." She leaned against him, putting her hand on his knee, her breast grazing his arm.

"There you go again! You just can't help yourself. I really

like you too, but can we take things a bit slower, please? You make me extremely nervous."

Both Camilla's and her grandmother's words popped into her head. "When he's the right one, you'll know."

"Deal," she said.

Turning into a small courtyard, the driver pulled the car up to the front door of a house. The door stood to the right side of a section that had once been a barn, and where a trellis of climbing roses obscured a faded sign that read, "*Luc Gaspard – Médecin Généraliste.*"

"Miss Smytheson?"

A big bear of a man stood at the threshold waiting to greet them. He grasped her hands between his own, kissing her on each cheek.

"I'm Jean-Luc. I'm so happy to meet you. Papa is waiting for you. *Éntrez.*"

On the other side of an open space living room, an elderly man struggled to stand from a chair by the fireplace. A heavy floral scent from the rose bush outside the front door flowed into the room.

"Hello," she said. Her knees were trembling as she walked towards him. "I believe you're my grandfather. I have something here that may bring back memories for you." She held out her grandmother's shoebox containing all the cherished mementos Eve had saved.

As he approached her, his tall figure bent over with age, Georgina looked into deep blue eyes that mirrored her own. They shone with the tenderness that her grandmother had described.

"I always knew my rose would come back to me one day." He reached for his granddaughter's hand, pulling her into his arms.

"She's never stopped loving you." Georgina's voice choked with emotion as she leaned against her grandfather's shoulder. "I'm so happy we've found you."

Luc noticed Paul standing alone in the doorway and waved for him to enter. "Come in, young man. You must be my granddaughter's husband."

Georgina blushed. "Oh no. This is my friend Paul. He's the man who helped me find you."

"Well, come and sit down, both of you, and tell me about my Eve. How is she?"

"She's very frail these days, but her mind is as sharp as a whip. She's told me about your love story and what happened during the war."

"It was a special love. Even my wife knew about Eve," Luc said, looking over towards his son. "I know she would be happy for me to have found her. And now I have the gift of a new granddaughter."

He eased himself down into his armchair, staring at the shoebox that sat on his lap, with a faraway look in his eyes.

"Monsieur Lacroix was a member of the Resistance too. Sadly, he died before he was recognized for his role in the war. I believe his grandson has carried on his trade, though. The shoe shop is still open today." He slowly opened the lid. Gently taking the pink glove in his hand, he pressed it to his face. Reaching into his pocket, he took out the other glove of the pair and placed them on top of each other. "I have kept this all my life, hoping beyond hope that they would be reunited one day."

Jean-Luc cleared his throat. "Can I get everyone something to drink? I think a toast is in order." He went out of the room and returned several minutes later with a tray of glasses and a bottle of champagne. He poured them each a glass before raising his own.

"Here's to Luc and Eve and to their future reunion, and to Providence that has brought us all together. This is an extraordinary day!"

He put his glass down, seeming to hesitate for a moment. He looked over at Luc, who nodded his head.

"We have some news to share with you. I'm sure your grandmother told you about the little boy she rescued, Jacob Halévy. Well, he's still alive and lives in America. Papa had told my mother and me about him. He'd discovered that Eve left Jacob in the care of the UNNC after the liberation of Grenoble, but there was no trace of anyone named Eve Charlot. We found out that an American family had adopted Jacob. They decided that he should keep his parents' name, so finding him wasn't so difficult. He lives in New York and has kept in touch with us over the years. I spoke to him yesterday. He would very much like to meet your grandmother."

Georgina waved her hand and her eyes flashed excitedly between Luc and his son. "Wait a minute! Jacob Halévy? I know someone called Jacob Halévy. Could he be the same Jacob who raises money for children's charities and for orphanages in the city? My Jacob has a wife called Sara. I've worked on a lot of fundraisers with them."

Paul stared at her in amazement. "You've never told me you volunteered for a charity. You've got to be kidding me! You know him?" he said.

"I can't be sure it's him."

Jean-Luc was listening to the exchange between Georgina and Paul.

"I think it could be him. Jacob's wife is called Sara. Since he retired, he's devoted his time to children's charities."

"It is him. It must be," Georgina said. "I remember him talking about a daughter called Eve and I told him that was my grandmother's name. Oh, my goodness. I think I'm going to faint."

Eve was very quiet for several minutes after Georgina gently broke the news to her that Luc was still alive. Georgina was concerned that the shock was too much for her frail constitution. The old woman was breathing rapidly, and her already pale face turned even whiter.

"Are you absolutely certain it's him?" Eve asked finally, her hands trembling as she removed her oxygen mask. "They told me he died."

"Of course, Grandy. But I had to be certain before I could tell you. That's why I went to France to meet him myself. I'm one hundred percent positive it's him. It was like looking into my own eyes, and he's definitely as gorgeous as you described him."

"Now you're making me nervous, dear. What's he going to think when he sees my old, shriveled face?" Eve touched Georgina's hand. "Thank you, my darling, for listening to an old woman. I can't describe how urgently I needed to tell my story. It was as if someone was pulling me into the past, encouraging me to unburden myself before I die, and you listened, you believed me. Yes, it was painful to tell, and the memories are so, so sad, but it was my life. And because of you, this miracle has happened. Luc's alive!"

"I know—I found a grandfather I never knew I had. And I found you too. I love you, Grandy."

Puffy clouds filled the October sky, with rain not far away. Paul had taken the long route from the airport, passing through Gloucester and Cheltenham before reaching Worcester. Luc sat next to him in the passenger seat. The old man didn't seem tired after his flight from Grenoble to London and was gazing at the view of the countryside as they drove along the country lanes.

"I've never been to England, you know," he said. "It's as

beautiful as I thought it would be."

"Where did you learn to speak such perfect English?"

"I learned as a child. It's come in useful over the years."

"This story goes from one irony to another. All those years ago Eve never knew you could speak her language so well."

Paul pulled into a parking space outside number thirty-two and switched off the engine.

"We're here. Are you ready?"

He noticed that Luc's hands were trembling slightly as he opened the car door.

"I feel like a young man again. My heart won't stop quivering and my mouth feels dry. I felt just like this when I first met her, you know," Luc said. He ran his hand slowly through his wiry grey hair and exhaled. "I just hope she still likes me!"

Paul gave him a reassuring pat on the shoulder. "It's a bit unsettling, isn't it? I know someone who makes me feel like that. Come on. Let's not keep her waiting any longer."

Earlier that morning, Georgina had helped Eve get ready for her reunion with Luc. She had styled the old lady's hair and helped her dress in a soft blue cotton dress with a single string of pearls at her neck. Eve glowed with happiness as they sat together in the garden.

The sun had come out at last, bathing Eve's flowers in afternoon light. Footsteps crunched on the gravel path. Eve looked up as a shadow fell across the lawn. The scent of late roses lingered in the air.

"Eve, it's really you," Luc whispered. "Your beautiful face is just the same as the morning I left you."

Georgina helped her grandmother to her feet. She held her breath as the old woman walked unaided towards him.

"Look," Eve said. "I'm not limping anymore. You fixed my leg."

She pulled out a tissue from the sleeve of her dress and reaching up, wiped away the tears that were trickling down

Luc's cheeks. "Oh, don't cry," she said.

"They're tears of happiness, my beautiful rose," Luc replied, looking down at her.

She gazed up at his face, studying every inch, every wrinkle, every crease, savoring the moment for which, until now, she had only dreamed about. Her eyes glistened. "Who would have thought my ancient old body could ever feel like this again. Oh, my Luc, you're here! All these years, I thought you were dead." Her bony hand reached out for his and grasped it as if she never wanted to let it go.

"I knew we would see each other one day; we were always meant to be together. But I never thought to look for you here. No one knew where you'd gone. I searched and searched," he said.

"They told me everyone in Vassieux was killed. I was pregnant and so sick. I came home to have our baby. I called her Angela."

"Angélique, that was my mother's name... Is my daughter here?

"No, but perhaps one day you'll meet her. Come, sit down and let me just look at you." Eve lay her head on his chest. A wisp of a breeze caressed their faces, the years and heartache melting away.

Georgina reached for Paul's hand and pulled him towards her. He brushed a tear off his face with his fingers and sniffed loudly.

"I love that you're such a romantic," she said. "It is an amazing love story."

Anyone else looking at the elderly couple holding hands on that autumn day could not possibly see what Georgina now knew: what they had experienced, suffered, endured. It wasn't just a love story, it was a tale of duty, sacrifice, survival, and much more. And it was a history that embraced her too; it told her where she had come from and the person she needed to be. It was the blood that ran through her veins. She'd found the family she didn't even know she'd been looking for.

"The story isn't finished yet," Paul said. His fingers brushed softly against hers.

"What do you think about meeting Jacob and Sara next week?" she asked.

"We found your grandfather because of the technology at our disposal these days. But you knowing Jacob is a twist of fate that's taken this narrative to another level," he replied.

"I know. I still can't believe it. I think…" Georgina gasped suddenly and touched her stomach.

"Are you okay?" Paul asked.

"Feel this," she said, excitedly grabbing his hand. "It's moving!"

"What is?"

"The baby. It's moving!"

"You're having a baby?

"Yes. A girl."

"Wow! You really are one for surprises. Does everyone else but me know?" He ruffled his hand through his hair with the confused look on his face that Georgina now found so endearing.

"Yes, everyone knows. I thought I'd scare you away if I told you."

"You're quite something! Is the baby's father in the picture?"

"No, not yet. But that's something I need to deal with. I don't want to tell him by email, or even on the phone. This is something we need to discuss face to face. I'd like him to be part of her life if he wants to be, but I don't expect anything from him. I'm not in love with him."

Georgina sat down heavily on the garden bench. Paul sat next to her and placed his hand on her stomach again.

"This little girl is going to be in for quite a ride with you as her mother. What are you going to do about your job?"

"I have to go back to New York to sort a lot of things out. I'm a mess, I know, but if you'll have me, this is where I really want to be." Georgina, for the first time in her life, felt shy. "I'm sorry I didn't tell you before. I hope you'll be here when I come back," she whispered.

He looked down at her and smiled.

"We'll see," he said. He pulled her close and kissed the top of her head. "As long as you promise the next time we go out for dinner, you won't order me a chicken vindaloo. With you around, I'm going to have more than enough excitement on my plate to deal with."

EPILOGUE

Ma Chérie,

My beautiful rose, I must go. Our time has come to fight. The Allies have landed in Normandy, and we must defend the region from the Germans. My sweet, brave, passionate Eve, I have loved you from the first moment I saw you. You are the air that surrounds me, caressing me, nurturing my heart, filling it with so much love that sometimes I feel it will burst with happiness. When you are in my arms it's like time has stopped and we're the only two alive. I don't know when I'll see you again, it may be in this world or the next, but I know that when we do meet again, my darling, it will be forever.

ACKNOWLEDGMENTS

A big thank-you to all the people who supported and encouraged me throughout the process of writing this book:

Michael Romano, whose editing helped me to prepare my manuscript for submission. You are brilliant and I couldn't have done this without you.

The team at Atmosphere Press. You've made my dream to become a published author a reality. Working with you all has been a pleasure.

Finally, my family and friends who have been my cheerleaders for the past three years. Your enduring enthusiasm and interest spurred me on through my moments of self-doubt. I'll always treasure your sensitive feedback and advice. You are too numerous to mention, but you know who you are. I cherish you all.

ABOUT ATMOSPHERE PRESS

Atmosphere Press is an independent, full-service publisher for excellent books in all genres and for all audiences. Learn more about what we do at atmospherepress.com.

We encourage you to check out some of Atmosphere's latest releases, which are available at Amazon.com and via order from your local bookstore:

Twisted Silver Spoons, a novel by Karen M. Wicks

Queen of Crows, a novel by S.L. Wilton

The Summer Festival is Murder, a novel by Jill M. Lyon

The Past We Step Into, stories by Richard Scharine

Swimming with the Angels, a novel by Colin Kersey

Island of Dead Gods, a novel by Verena Mahlow

Twins Daze, a novel by Jerry Petersen

Abaddon Illusion, a novel by Lindsey Bakken

Blackland: A Utopian Novel, by Richard A. Jones

The Jesus Nut, a novel by John Prather

The Embers of Tradition, a novel by Chukwudum Okeke

Saints and Martyrs: A Novel, by Aaron Roe

When I Am Ashes, a novel by Amber Rose

The Recoleta Stories, by Bryon Esmond Butler

Voodoo Hideaway, a novel by Vance Cariaga

Hart Street and Main, a novel by Tabitha Sprunger

The Weed Lady, a novel by Shea R. Embry

A Book of Life, a novel by David Ellis

It Was Called a Home, a novel by Brian Nisun

Grace, a novel by Nancy Allen